Blood Bred Series, Book 1:
Gift of Blood

By JennaKay Francis

Writers Exchange E-Publishing

http://www.writers-exchange.com

My life had been the sun but now I have no choice to be who I am. After all these years I notice that to the lonely moon there are also stars in the sky. A single, bright star will affect my existence. Rhiannon. She shows me that the moon is actually not an enemy but a companion.

> *--Toni Griffing*

Jaeger looked down at his hands. They were shaking. Hell, his whole body was shaking. His gaze moved to the unconscious young boy sprawled on the ground. This was insane; totally mad. Jaeger raked one hand through his hair and took several steps away.

His gaze swept over the surrounding fields. Grazing land, mostly, but a thick copse of maple trees stood on either side of the lane, plunging it into cool, blue-black darkness. The trees had hidden Jaeger, and he spooked the child's horse when he stepped into the open without warning. Now, guilt raged through him as he once more approached the unconscious youth.

How could I have done this? He's a child, just a child. Still...

He hunkered down beside the boy band ran one long, slender finger along the child's neck. The skin was soft and warm; the vein pulsed with each heartbeat.

Jaeger's mouth watered at the thought of the blood surging through it, back and forth, never ceasing, giving life...

A soft moan startled him. He drew back as the boy roused.

"What happened?" The child's voice was groggy.

"You fell from your horse," Jaeger said with a calm he didn't feel.

The boy glanced at the horse grazing nearby. "I've never fallen before."

"Perhaps my sudden appearance alongside the road frightened your animal."

The boy shot another quick glance at the horse, then looked back at Jaeger. "Who are you? What are you doing here?"

"I'm but a passerby."

"You're trespassing," the boy snapped, getting unsteadily to his feet.

Jaeger lifted his eyebrows in surprise. "Oh? I saw no boundary signs."

The boy sneered at him. "You imbecile! Everyone knows these lands belong to Lord Dain." He brushed his leathers clean with disgusted short strokes.

"Ah, Lord Dain. Then you must be his heir, Fellowes." Jaeger regarded him thoughtfully. He was a nice-looking boy with a mop of golden hair and wide, expressive brown eyes. His clothing was expensive, his boots of the finest leather. He wore a gold crest ring on his smallest finger and some sort of gold medallion about his neck. Overall, he seemed the picture of innocence. So, his next words surprised Jaeger.

"You're not as stupid as you look," he said.

Jaeger drew a slow breath, holding back his irritation. "As far as stupidity goes, I am not the one falling from my horse."

Anger reddened Fellowes' face. He stomped over to the horse. "Well, it'll be the last time this old nag throws me!" He snatched his riding crop from its holder on the saddle, and before Jaeger could stop him, brought the whip down sharply against the horse's flank.

The animal cried out in pain, attempting to dance aside, but Fellowes had a tight grip on its halter. He raised his hand to deliver another blow.

Jaeger leapt forward, seized Fellowes' wrist and tore the crop away from him.

"How dare you!" Fellowes raged.

"No. How dare *you*?" Jaeger countered, his voice cold and soft. "The horse was not at fault here. She deserves no punishment."

Fellowes struggled against Jaeger's grip. "She will be punished if I say she will. She's my horse."

"No longer." With his free hand, Jaeger removed the horse's halter and loosened the saddle girth. A sharp slap on the rump sent the animal bolting, rearing, and kicking to escape the saddle. It hit the ground with a solid thud, and the mare tore away into the surrounding grasslands.

Fellowes gasped in open disbelief. "Who the hell do you think you are? My father is going to hear about this. And when he does, your life will be forfeit."

Jaeger paused, his grip on the boy's wrist tightening. "No, I think not," he said softly, then drew the boy close, his mouth hungry for the pulsing vein and the blood therein.

Jaeger hunched into his black cloak, keeping his gaze on his half-empty stein. The large pub was crowded and noisy. Pipe smoke mixed with that from the hearth and mingled with the scents of goat stew, ale, and sweat. The unpleasant stench settled on Jaeger's clothes, crawled through his hair, and coated his tongue. He took another long pull from his stein to drown out the taste.

Several dozen men, mostly local herdsmen, gathered about him, boisterous and excited. Jaeger listened to their words, his heart pounding. Lord Dain's son had been found dead alongside the trail just hours earlier, his body drained of blood. There had been no signs of a duel, no outward injury to the boy, save for several small puncture wounds on his neck. Word had traveled fast through the small hamlet, and settled on the Vectors, the "undead" who wandered the land searching for human blood to quench their thirst.

Lord Dain had sent his best men in search of the killer, and had offered a generous reward for capture of the same. The village men discussed forming groups and argued over how the reward money would be split.

Jaeger winced at the open hostility and disdain coloring the men's words. Their hatred of Vectors was very apparent. He took another drink and slouched further into his cloak. His only saving grace was that he had arrived in this village some weeks past and the consensus among the vigilantes seemed to be that they were looking for a stranger. And with his Illusion, that of an aged man barely capable of walking, he was quickly discounted as a suspect.

Still, he wished he could stand up for himself, for his kind. Not all Vectors were murderers. In fact, Jaeger could tick off on one hand those Vectors he considered truly evil.

If there was evil in anyone, it was in the humans. They were the ones hunting down Vectors, as if in sport. They had discovered Vector vulnerabilities, the ways they could be killed. That the death was torture for the victim didn't seem to matter to those humans seeking their demise.

Most Vectors wanted only to live in peace, surviving the best they could on a diet requiring blood. Most Vectors didn't kill their victims, either. They didn't need that much blood. Why Fellowes was dead was a mystery. Jaeger certainly would never kill a child. He hadn't taken enough to kill the boy.

Why he had taken any blood at all was a question that pounded through his mind. He had always quenched his thirst with goat's blood, easily obtainable in the pastures spread out over the countryside. At least, he had until now.

Whatever had possessed him today? What had made him turn on a human for the first time in his very long life? He shook his head and took another pull from his stein.

"Ah, Jaeger." The voice seemed loud, even in the noisy room. "You're the last person I'd expect to find here."

Jaeger looked up in astonishment. "Celd!"

He was shocked to see him here, though Jaeger was not surprised Celd had found him. Vectors had a way of honing in on their own kind, and Celd seemed more adept than most. Jaeger supposed it had something to do with the fact that they really had no others they could call friend or family.

Not that he considered Celd a friend. Quite the opposite; Jaeger had always seen him as pompous, aloof and...cruel. When Jaeger's parents had died and he had gone to live in the Lair, he often found himself the victim of the other Vector's jibes.

Celd could afford to look down his nose at him. His father was not only a Chosen, but also one of the Sovereign's closest aides. *His* father, unlike Jaeger's, had not been banished from the Lair, condemned for loving a mere human.

His father had not conceived a son who was ashamed of his heritage.

Jaeger sighed. When had he become so disgusted with himself?

Celd collapsed onto the bench opposite him. They were both under Illusion, as was custom in public. Tonight, custom called for the world to see them as two bent and aged men. It would not have been so easy to overlook them had they appeared as themselves; most Vectors stood more than six feet tall, tended to have raven-black hair, sharp features, and almond-shaped black eyes set into skin the color of porcelain. Their frames were lean but muscular, and their bearing regal.

They were not easily forgotten.

"So," Celd said, gesturing at the other patrons and speaking to Jaeger in their own tongue, "I see you've been busy."

"I didn't kill him," Jaeger said, his grip tightening on his stein.

Celd chuckled and took a drink from his own stein. "No, of course you didn't. There was never any doubt in my mind."

Jaeger looked at him sharply, catching the meaning in the words. "You?"

Celd shrugged. "I was hungry. Besides, he was an insolent little cur. Sharp-tongued and dull-witted. If anyone deserved to die, it was him."

Jaeger shuddered and averted his gaze. "He was a child."

"He was delicious," Celd countered.

Jaeger sucked in an angry breath but did no more than tighten his jaw and change the subject. "What brings you out here? I thought you despised the country."

"I do," Celd admitted. "But I was on the trail of a Bleeder. Would've found her, too, but the fresh blood of the boy interfered."

"A Bleeder? Out here?" Jaeger looked up at him. "Besides, I thought you had one back in the city."

"She died." Celd slouched nonchalantly into his chair and took another drink.

Jaeger studied him in disgust. "You bled her to death, just like the others." He shook his head.

"It was an accident," Celd told him. "We got a little carried away. One thing led to another."

"It usually is an accident with you. How many does that make now?"

"I'm not keeping count. Are you?"

Jaeger ignored the sarcasm and huddled even further into his cloak.

"Well, look at that," Celd murmured, his gaze shifting across the crowded room.

Jaeger looked up in time to see the bar wench deliver a round of drinks to a nearby table. Her bodice was laced tight over generous breasts that threatened to spill out of their confines. Long, golden locks were gathered in a loose braid reaching halfway down her back. Soft, pink lips pulled back in a genuine smile, revealing flawless white teeth. Her blue eyes sparkled in the lamplight as she glanced toward Jaeger and Celd.

Celd smiled, but Jaeger reached across the table and gripped his arm. "Leave her alone, Celd. You don't need to feed again."

Celd chuckled. "You just don't understand, do you, Jaeg? It's not a question of need. It's a question of want." He rose. "Excuse me. I have dinner reservations to make."

Jaeger watched him saunter away, knowing he would change his appearance, then make his move on the barmaid. Jaeger downed the last of his drink and rose as well. He would be no part of it. He made his way to the door of the pub and stepped into the cold night air. He sniffed the air to separate and distinguish the various scents oozing from the darkness as he thought about what Celd had said.

A Bleeder? In this area? Why hadn't he noticed? Had his self-enforced diet of goat's blood affected his Vector senses that much? He should have been able to smell the iron.

Celd had mentioned it was female. A woman, or a girl? A child? Jaeger didn't think that Celd would bother with a child. He tended to seek out those of the female gender old enough to show him a good time before he drained them of their life's fluid. The boy had been a diversion, a temptation Celd had not been able to resist. Therefore, this Bleeder he was looking for was a woman, at least 18 years of age.

Jaeger walked away from the pub, keeping his senses alert. The pipe and wood smoke still clung to him, making his assessment of the surrounding area difficult. He noticed nothing more than the usual--grass, trees, goats, along with all of the various scents associated with the pub he had left behind.

With a heavy sigh, he turned his steps toward the small village of Skyther and his temporary home there at the inn. This was what he hated most about being a Vector--no sense of place. He never stayed long at one village, worried that suspicious fingers would begin to point his way. It was one thing to lose a goat or two to bloodthirsty predators; but when the losses continued, people looked for a reason. Jaeger didn't want to be that reason. He had seen what happened to those accused of being a "blood-eater". Thinking of it made him shudder, and he quickened his pace.

As he rounded a corner leading to the dark alleyway alongside the inn, a familiar scent cut through the night air. Jaeger stopped, the pupils of his dark eyes widening like a cat's, taking in what little light there was.

Blood. Freshly spilled blood. Human blood.

A tremor ran through him. A tremor of excitement. He squelched it with a grimace. One human. He'd had only one human, and already he was yearning for more. He shook the thought aside and kept walking.

The smell grew stronger. It wafted through the alley, floated on the air, wrapped around him like a lover's embrace. Warm, sensual, exotic, alluring. Jaeger could not resist it, didn't want to. He let it lead him forward, out of the alley, across a deserted street, to an empty warehouse by the wharves.

Black lake water lapped quietly against weathered wood as it pawed at the stony shore like an animal stripped of its claws. Jaeger pulled his cloak tighter, keeping well away from the edges of the tilting docks. He hated water when he couldn't see what lay beneath its surface. Still, the blood scent was coming from down there, under the wooden slats on which he stood. He paused, heart pounding, keeping time with the *shush, shush* of the waves.

He wanted to turn, to go back, to settle into his lumpy bed and take what sleep this night would afford him. But, at the same time, he was drawn to the scent. Carefully, he retraced his steps until he found easy access to the shore. Once there, he hesitated, drawing a deep breath. Brine, oil, tar--and blood. They combined into an alluring potpourri. Jaeger closed his eyes, trying to dispel the urgency tugging him forward.

After a moment, he moved back toward the docks, his gaze searching the black pit beneath. The scent was stronger now, almost overwhelming. It was young, warm, and full of life. Yet, at the same time, Jaeger knew its source was dying. As it flowed, the blood pooled in the dark rocks, chilling, mixing with the fetid waters, lost forever to both him and its host. The thought almost angered Jaeger. Almost. He was still far enough removed from Blood Thirst to be concerned about the wellbeing of whomever was bleeding so profusely.

He crouched, holding on to the coarse wood for balance.

Jaeger saw her now; a frail form huddled into a corner, limp and unconscious. It took him only a moment to reach her side, to find the source of her injury. A gash crossed her left wrist. Blood flowed out, crawled across her small hand, and dripped into the rocks beneath her. He pulled his kerchief from his pocket, lifted her arm, and wrapped the wound, intent upon stanching the incessant flow of blood. His hands shook. Warm blood touched his skin; the scent assailed his nostrils, and captured his gaze. Black and shiny in the absence of direct light, the blood looked like a glittering jewel against the girl's white skin.

Jaeger forced his gaze to her face. She was young. She was beautiful. She was covered with filth. Her head was tipped back, her dark hair fell to one side. Her slender white neck tilted alluringly, enticing him closer. He set his jaw. He had promised. Jaeger had made a vow to his mother so many years ago. Goat's blood would be his diet. Goat's blood. Not human. Not ever human.

A soft, shuddering sob escaped him. He had broken that vow, drawn by some unexplainable force. He had tasted human blood. He had enjoyed it. Even now, it coursed through his body, making him feel young and vibrant. Alive. So alive. Goat's blood had never done that, could never do that. Now...lying here before him, like an offering, was this sweet, young human. Here for the taking. He had only to bend his head, take what was left. No one would know. If her body were found at all, it wouldn't be in any shape anyone could recognize.

She moaned softly. Her eyes fluttered open, as if uncertain they could still do so. A lightning-blue gaze met his black one. "Help me," she whispered. "Please, help me."

Jaeger paused before the closed door. A tray rested lightly on the palm of one hand, the offerings on it warm and fragrant. Soup and tea; just the thing to help the young woman recover her strength.

Jaeger had brought her to his room at the inn. He had slid in through a back door, taken a servant's stairway to his floor, and crept like a wraith down the dark hallway to his room. Once there, he stripped her of her wet and bloody clothes, working quickly to limit the amount of time his hands touched her young, supple flesh. What he originally thought was mud and grime he now saw were bruises in various stages of healing. The thought sickened him. He would never understand how humans could inflict such pain on each other.

She did not stir while he tended her injuries and cleaned the dirt from her bruised flesh. Once she was dry and warm beneath the covers on his bed, she sank into what appeared to be a deeper rest.

Jaeger stoked the fireplace, wrote her a brief message in case she should awaken, then left to find his own dinner. It had been a true test of his willpower--and his vow to his deceased mother--that the young woman had not provided that dinner.

Satiated, he returned, bringing food for the young woman though he was not even sure if she would still be in the room. Drawing a deep breath, he turned the handle, pushed open the door, and let himself in.

The room was warm and dark, the only light coming from the fireplace. Jaeger chastised himself for not leaving the lamp burning. With his exquisite night vision, he often forgot. Quietly, he closed the door, placed the tray of food on the side table, and went to the fireplace to fetch a taper for the lamp.

"Hello." Her voice was a whisper of warm air through the darkness.

Jaeger turned, able to see her quite clearly despite the dim light. She was sitting up in bed, the covers drawn up against her throat. Her dark hair fell limply against her thin face, framing eyes that seemed too large for her small stature. Jaeger smiled, then realized that she probably couldn't see him. Carefully, he took a bit of flaming wood and lit the lamp. It shed a yellow glow over the room.

The woman let out a small gasp.

Jaeger felt color rush to his cheeks, and he averted his gaze, wondering at this new emotion swelling inside him. "I'm sorry. I startled you."

"No," she said quickly, then, "Yes, you did. I guess I wasn't expecting a...well, a man to be my savior."

A man, Jaeger thought to himself. He grimaced, a touch of panic sweeping through him. This was the first time he had actually forgotten to Illusion, to disguise himself as someone other than who and what he was. Still, she did not seem unduly alarmed by his Vector appearance. Perhaps, however improbable it was, she was unaware of them.

He gestured toward the tray. "I've brought you some soup and tea."

She looked at the food. "Thank you." Her voice was barely above a whisper. "And have I you to thank for the...well, the..." Her words trailed off as her gaze slid to the bedclothes covering her nudity.

Again, Jaeger's cheeks burned. "You...you were wet," he stammered. He moved toward the tray, amazed he didn't trip over his own feet. "Here. You need to get some warmth inside of you." He placed the tray of food on the chair beside the bed, then backed away.

She looked up at him. "I'm left-handed," she said softly.

At first, her meaning was lost on Jaeger. She gave a small smile and held up her bandaged hand.

"Oh," Jaeger murmured. "I...oh." He pulled another chair close to the bed and took up a spoonful of the soup, chagrined to see his hand was trembling.

He placed the spoon near her lips, suddenly noticing how full and pink they were. He swallowed at the same time she did, though it wasn't soup washing down his throat. It was lust, pure and simple. His entire body was reacting to her closeness, something that had never happened before. He scooped another spoonful of the soup and fed it to her, trying to keep his gaze from her face. He was well aware of her eyes on him, however, watching his every move. It seemed to take an eternity to empty the soup bowl, but when he finally did, he got up with a haste born of desperation.

"I'll just return this tray to the kitchen." His voice sounded husky and unnatural.

"My tea?"

"Oh. Yes. Here." He placed the cup on the side table. "I'll be right back."

"I'll be here," she replied, a small smile touching at her mouth.

Jaeger took a deep breath, almost choking on it. He picked up the tray and made quick, calculated movements to get himself out of the room. Once in the hallway, he leaned against the closed door with a sigh. What was happening? Why was he reacting like this? He had known dozens of women in his lifetime, some more beautiful than the woman in his room, some less so. But none, not one, had ever affected him like this.

He set the tray on the floor and headed toward the back staircase. He needed to get into the cold night air. With a grimace, he slipped down the stairs and melted into the dark alley behind the inn. A brisk walk to the main street did much to restore his usual calm.

His gaze traveled the unlit streets. He could sense Celd was near, though he didn't see the man. Probably bedding down the barmaid, Jaeger thought with disgust. Then he would bleed her, every day, until she, too, succumbed to death. Jaeger wished there was something he could do, but he knew there wasn't. He had tried to talk women away from such possessive Vectors before. It was impossible. Once they were under the Vector spell, they were there until death released them.

Jaeger often wondered what became of those who died in such a way. Rumors when he was younger suggested the dead became Vectors. Jaeger had never seen evidence of it. But, then, he had never searched out a victim, either. He considered what might happen if Fellowes should turn into a Vector, come after him for revenge. The thought sent a cold shudder racing through Jaeger, and he quickly scanned his surroundings as if expecting Fellowes to leap out at him.

Instead, he saw Celd. The Vector was dabbing delicately at his mouth with his kerchief. Jaeger saw fresh bloodstains on the white cloth. His mouth watered as strange longings rushed through him. It was with a great degree of difficulty that he pushed them aside.

"Good eve," he said quietly.

Celd chuckled, replacing his kerchief into his vest pocket. "Indeed it was. The barmaid is quite the charmer. I should get to the country more often."

Jaeger tensed. "Is she...dead?"

"Dead?" Celd seemed truly appalled by the question. "Of course she's not dead. I only took what I needed. She's sleeping it off."

"Where?"

"At the inn. I procured a room. Did you think I was going to bed her here in the alley?" He laughed. "And what are you doing here?"

Jaeger shrugged, his brow furrowing with concern. He didn't like the idea that Celd was in the same inn as he. He sought to direct the conversation away from his insecurities. "Celd, may I ask you something?" Though he was loath to converse with Celd in a friendly manner, there was no one else he could turn to at the moment. And there were questions to which he desperately needed answers.

Celd bobbed his head. "Certainly. What plagues your mind tonight?"

Jaeger took a deep breath and plunged on. "You know me. You know my tastes. Yet, today, for the first time, I hungered for human blood. Me. Jaeger. The Goat Vector." He gave a wry grin at Celd's look of surprise. "Yes, I know the names I have been called. Goat Vector. Goat Boy. The Horned One. Human halfling. There are probably more. It doesn't matter. It was my choice. But, now...something has changed. I can't explain it."

Celd chuckled and placed one long arm about Jaeger's shoulders. "That's an easy one, Jaeg. You're growing up."

"Growing up?" Jaeger cast him a sour look, slipping free of his touch.

"Yes. Becoming a man, Jaeg, or, in this case, a real Vector."

Jaeger realized Celd was not teasing. He eyed the older man questioningly. "What does that mean?"

"All Vectors develop an increase in their thirst at about the same time they become able to father children. It's a natural process of growth, Jaeger. Revel in it."

Jaeger stared at him in astonishment. "But... I thought that...well, that Sovereign Cardiss was the father of all Vectors."

"You haven't been studying your heritage," Celd scolded. He moved away from Jaeger to lean against the stonewall of the closest building.

"I admit it. I had no interest in my heritage. But, now, well, suddenly it seems important."

"Ah, that taste of human blood you got earlier has awakened a new passion within you, hasn't it? I must say I am surprised you are experiencing this need at all, you with your human half. Still, your father's blood does flow through you. That must count for something." He pushed away from the wall. "Well, then, I'll tell you, Jaeg. But not here. I'm feeling a little full at the moment. Why don't we take a walk?" He started away.

Jaeger hesitated, his thoughts flying to the woman in his room. He had told her he would be back in a moment. It had already been much more than that. Still, he yearned to hear what Celd had to say. He nodded and fell into step beside the Vector.

They walked at a steady pace until they were clear of the village. Celd's path led them toward the lake, which sparkled as if embedded with tiny candles in the moonlight. "You see," Celd began as they stepped onto the rocky beach, "you were partially right in your statement. It is the Sovereign's seed that brings forth the new and pure Vectors. He creates an embryo using the seed from a Vector woman. That embryo is then implanted in one of the Chosen. You do know of the Chosen, don't you?"

Certainly, Jaeger had heard the word Chosen before, but he had never really understood the connotation of the word. Chancellor Riden, Celd's father, was one of the Chosen.

Celd continued, with a shake of his head at Jaeger's silence. "The

Chosen are hand-selected by the Sovereign. When the Chosen finds a suitable hostess, he then implants the embryo. His seed mixes with that of the human hostess, creating an atmosphere in which the embryo can take root and grow. In that way, though the pure Vector is a child of the Sovereign, he or she is also the child of the Chosen and the hostess. In essence, we have two fathers and two mothers."

"Why a birth hostess? Why not just allow Vector women to carry the child?"

Celd shot him a glance. "You really haven't studied at all, have you? A female Vector does not carry a child, Jaeger. It's been this way for centuries. Vectors found early on that humans were better designed for propagating their species--and ours. There is something in their human blood that gives strength to a Vector child. It continues to give strength after the birth. When the child is born, the hostess provides its first taste of blood."

Jaeger stared at the water before him, the words swirling in his head. He was almost afraid to ask his next question, yet needed to know. He drew a deep breath. "The hostess, what becomes of her?"

Celd shrugged. "She is bled. Some of her blood feeds the infant for a week or so, the rest goes to the Chosen."

Jaeger looked at him, his heart aching. "So, she dies, then?"

"She must. She has fulfilled her purpose. And we can't have a multitude of women running around screaming about missing babies, now, can we?" He laughed, obviously amused at the look of disgust and despair that Jaeger could not suppress. He reached over and squeezed Jaeger's neck. "I swear, Jaeger, you must have gotten some human breast milk when you were born."

"Breast milk? What do you mean?"

"Surest way to kill the Vector element in a newborn," Celd replied, then added, mockingly, "Or maybe someone slipped you some goat's milk."

Jaeger reddened at Celd's sarcastic laughter and drew the neck of his tunic closer. "My mother was human," he said softly. "She wasn't a hostess. So, why was she killed?"

Celd snorted with annoyance. "She was a human, trying to raise a Vector son. Sovereign Cardiss thinks highly of all of his children, but the boys more so."

"But I am not one of his children," Jaeger pointed out. "My father was not a Chosen."

"But *his* father was. Through that bloodline, you belong to Cardiss, just as we all do."

The words made Jaeger shudder. "I'm cold, Celd. I think I'll return to my room, now. Thank you for the information."

"You're welcome." Celd hesitated, peering at him intently. "Sure you won't make a visit to the barmaid as well? She's a delicate little piece."

Jaeger felt his cheeks flush as he turned away. "No, thank you. Besides, if I know you, you've worked your own brand of charm on her. She'll have no other."

Celd laughed. "You are so right, my young friend. I'll walk you back."

"No, that's not necessary. I...I need to think. Alone. Goodnight, Celd." Jaeger turned away, but Celd's grip stopped him.

"Do remember one thing, Jaeg," the Vector said. "Now that you've tasted human blood and entered the Growth, you'll need to be careful of direct sunlight. It's not a nice feeling. Your half human constitution might protect you, but are you willing to risk the pain to find out?"

Jaeger started at the warning and pulled away from Celd's grasp. "I'll remember that, Celd. Thank you."

He strode away, his mind awash with the new information. It was information that ate at his heart. So, this, then, was why his mother had been hunted down and killed, why his father had chosen the path he had?

Simply because his father had dared to impregnate a human, then allowed her to live after the birth of the child? Jaeger knew his father had defied the Sovereign, but he hadn't known to what extent. Still, to kill someone as beautiful and kind as his mother for no other reason than social habit....Jaeger shuddered.

His early youth had been spent moving, always moving. Sometimes without a moment's notice. He had resented it, hated the way it tore him away from familiar surroundings. Hated the fact that he could never make friends, never call a place home.

Time and again, he had asked for an explanation. Always, his parents had said it was not his concern, that he was too young to worry over the reasons. Nevertheless, he had worried. He had seen the fear in his father's eyes, the quiet resignation in his mother's. It suddenly occurred to Jaeger that she had known all along there was no escaping the Sovereign. She had known all along they would be found. He finally understood why his parents had pushed him to early self-sufficiency, had never really allowed him to be a child.

He had been handed responsibility at an early age, had been instilled with a sense of independence, while at the same time being sequestered from the reasons. It had not made sense then, but now he understood. Now, he wished he could reclaim those days, not be so angry and judgmental of his parents.

Jaeger stopped and turned his face to the heavens. He told himself that his parents were there, together, in a beautiful place where they no longer had to flee.

"I'm sorry," he whispered to the cold night air. "I am so sorry."

Jaeger tossed another log onto the fire, then sat back in his chair, wrapping the blanket tighter about his shoulders. Though the flame burned hot, he still shivered. He closed his eyes and leaned his head back against the chair. A cool hand on his forehead brought him alert with a gasp.

"I'm sorry. I didn't mean to startle you."

Jaeger swallowed hard, moving away from her touch. "No, it's all right, Rhiannon." He forced a smile to his lips. "You shouldn't be out of bed."

She smiled. "Nonsense. I feel quite well. But you look like you're ill. I want to help."

"No!" His answer was quick and adamant. He flushed when he saw the hurt and question enter her blue eyes. "I just mean I'm all right. Really. I'm just...cold. It's nothing."

Rhiannon hesitated, chewing thoughtfully on her lower lip. "If I go to the market, I could get some herbs that might help you."

"No," he said again, but this time the firm tone was meant. "No. You told me yourself how dangerous the market can be."

"But, Jaeger," she argued, "I want to help you. Just as you helped me. Please, let me do something."

He smiled at her. "You have done something, Rhiannon. You've given me incredible company this past week. Someone to talk to, to laugh with. I haven't had that for a long time." He took a risk and reached up to pat her arm.

As always, touching her sent emotions rushing through him, emotions he could no longer deny. Celd's words had embedded themselves in his mind. He wanted Rhiannon, wanted her in a carnal sense. It was all he could do to keep himself away from her as she slept. In fact, that was what had likely caused his illness. He forced himself to leave the room at night, to wander about in the dark and cold like some abandoned animal. During the day he napped, stretched out before the fire, in between caring for her and attending to her needs. But each time he touched her, felt her soft skin, he wanted her. Now, the lust was no less, and he drew away.

Rhiannon paused a moment longer, then abruptly knelt before him. She reached up and clasped his hand in hers. Her blue eyes were pleading, but before she could say a word, Jaeger gently pushed her aside and rose.

"I...I need to go out for a while," he managed. He snatched up his cloak and headed toward the door.

"Do you want me to leave?"

Her words stopped him in mid-stride. It was a moment before he could answer. He kept his gaze averted when he did. "I cannot tell you what to do," he said softly. "I think you still need time to recover from your injuries, but only you can say if you feel well enough to be on your own."

"That's not a response to what I asked you."

Jaeger drew a slow breath, swallowed, then turned to face her. As always, he felt his heart rate quicken and his body respond. Embarrassed, he pulled his cloak closer. "No, Rhiannon," he rasped. "No, I do not want you to leave." He spun, threw open the door and escaped into the hallway.

He took only a moment to gather his wits, to reinforce the Illusion of a middle-aged man, a persona he had used before in the village. Illusioning was always a hard press for him. He supposed it had to do with his human half. Still, he had become quite capable over the years. The only thing that threatened it was fatigue or distraction. Which would explain why he had failed to appear in Illusion before Rhiannon.

Satisfied his image was securely in place, he hurried down the back staircase for the security of the alley. He had spent a lot of time here in the past week, using it as a refuge from his own wild and turbulent emotions. Now, however, it did not offer him solace. Almost unconsciously, he turned his steps toward the tavern.

Rhiannon had told him how she came to be under the dock, about the men who had inflicted her injuries. Now, as he walked, he kept a sharp eye out for any of them, though Rhiannon had assured him that they had long since left the village. Anger burned in Jaeger's gut, mixing with the lust and the want. He needed some way to free these emotions, to expel them from his body. But how?

He pounded into the tavern, taking a seat in the corner. The barkeep glanced over at him, and he nodded, indicating that he would take an ale. It was brought quickly, and he downed a long pull before tossing several silvers on the wooden table. The barkeep scooped them up, a broad smile on his jowled face. Jaeger knew the brew would flow fast, keeping his tankard full. He took another long drink, then let his gaze wander over the other patrons.

Herders, most of them, still wearing the dirt and smell of their trade, Jaeger decided as he wrinkled his nose in disgust. Nowhere did he see the men Rhiannon had described to him. He knew a little of what they had done to her, how they had beaten her when she fought their advances. Rhiannon hadn't gone into detail. Jaeger hadn't pressed her. He knew only that they had finally let her go, battered and bleeding. That she had made it to the dock was evidence of her own strength; that she had held out as long as she had, was proof of her spirit and will.

Jaeger took another drink and slouched back against the rough wall. Absently, he wondered where Celd was. He had not seen the Vector or the barmaid for several days. The thought sent a shudder through him. He tuned his ear for any word of the girl's death, but the talk in the tavern that night seemed to be centered on the arrival of a gypsy caravan. Words of condemnation, mostly, from the same men who would later plunk down their coin to have their palms read or their fortunes scryed in some glass orb. With a shake of his head, Jaeger turned, slouching over his tankard.

"Good eve, m'lord." A slender young man slid onto the bench beside Jaeger, eyeing him with open interest. "Might I interest m'lord in a massage?"

Jaeger shook his head. "No. I'm fine."

"You look tense, m'lord. I've been told that I have the gift of healing in my hands. At the least, a sample of my handiwork before you say no." He slipped behind Jaeger and began to work the muscles in Jaeger's shoulders with firm, even strokes.

Despite himself, Jaeger relaxed. His eyelids dropped wearily, his fatigue catching up with him. The young man continued to work his own brand of magic, supple hands moving along Jaeger's neck, his shoulders, and his back. Jaeger felt himself leaning into the boy's massage. He finished off his tankard of ale. It was immediately refilled by the barkeep, who flashed a quick smile at the boy then disappeared. Jaeger knew he was being set up. He had seen the ploy before. Still, who was he to condemn the boy for trying to make a bit of money? Jaeger had to admit the boy was very gifted.

"How much will this cost me?" he murmured.

"Cost, m'lord? The pleasure is mine in seeing you enjoy my work."

Jaeger huffed out a little breath and took another pull from his tankard. His head was beginning to spin from the effects of the alcohol. He closed his eyes and let his mind wander. His thoughts immediately went to Rhiannon, and a small smile caught at his lips. She was beautiful. So exquisitely beautiful. How was he ever going to keep his hands from her? One of them would have to leave. That was sure. He didn't want to abandon her in this village that had caused her so much pain already. Still, how could he travel with her? The two of them, alone, on the road? He would never be able to control himself, not just in lust of her body, but in want of her blood.

He had not tasted human blood since his encounter with Fellowes, but it had not been easy to deny his yearning for it. If what Celd said was true, his yearnings would only grow stronger; and if Rhiannon was the only human within his reach...He shook himself and took another long drink.

"M'lord," the boy purred into his ear, "we could make this much more effective if you had a place to stretch out." He rose and took Jaeger by the arm, pulling him from his seat. "Come with me. I know just the place."

Head swirling, Jaeger drained the last of his tankard and allowed the boy to lead him from the tavern. They walked a short distance to the stables, where Jaeger stopped in confusion.

"In there?" he slurred.

The boy nodded. "I've a place all set up. You'll see. It's quite comfortable." He pulled Jaeger into the building, past a long set of stalls to one in the very back.

Jaeger, with his nightsight, took in the thick pile of hay overlaid with a large, soft blanket. The boy moved in front of him.

"My name is Shad," he said softly. His hands moved against Jaeger's cloak, pushing it aside. A second later, he had loosed the belt about Jaeger's tunic.

It was only then that Jaeger realized they were not alone. A movement, caught from the corner of his eye, drew his attention. Another youth, stouter than Shad and armed with something short and thick, stole from the darkness. Before Jaeger could react, the youth swung his weapon, striking Jaeger soundly on the side of the head.

Though he was stunned from the impact, Jaeger's Vector strength prevented him from being knocked unconscious, a fact that seemed to surprise and alarm his attacker. The youth stumbled back a step, even as Shad's hands closed about Jaeger's clothing.

"Hit him again!" Shad commanded, his voice no longer quiet and soothing.

Jaeger swung out one arm, catching the other youth at neck level. The boy crumpled to the hay, knocked cold by the powerful blow. Shad started, his gaze darting from his friend to Jaeger.

Fury allowed the Illusion he had created to fade, revealing his true appearance to Shad. The boy gasped and backed away, as if hoping to disappear into the darkness. Jaeger paced him step for step, until there was no place left for Shad to go. The youth pressed against the rough, wooden walls and looked up at Jaeger, pleading in his dark eyes.

"M'lord, please," he whispered, "forgive me. It...it's not what you think."

"Not what I think?" Jaeger repeated, forcing the ill effects from the ale aside. "You have the barkeep fill me with drink, you lure me here where your friend waits to smash my skull so that you may rob me of what you think I have. Or were you only attempting to gain my favors sexually?" He lifted his hand and traced one long finger down the side of Shad's face.

Shad trembled. "N...no, m'lord. No. That's not it at all. I...I don't lean toward men."

"Well," Jaeger murmured, gripping the back of Shad's neck in a firm grip, "what if I do? You've a pleasant enough face. Maybe I should see the rest of you as well."

It was all Jaeger could do to keep from laughing as he watched the color drain from Shad's face. He could have taken the deception further, could have ordered the boy to strip, to parade before him, could have forced him to do any number of things. However, at that moment, his gaze rested on the boy's neck, on the pulsing artery that surged with youth and vitality. Yes, he wanted this boy, but not for the reasons he was suggesting.

The boy went rigid in Jaeger's grasp, pressing his back against the wall. He lifted one arm as if to push Jaeger away, then dropped it back to his side. His gaze was locked on Jaeger's, his mind controlled by the hypnotic influence of a Vector.

Jaeger's anger and need rushed through him, set his heart racing, his pulse pounding. Every part of his body was responding to this boy before him, this warm, human boy who held such vast stores of red life. Jaeger didn't even care that he was fully erect, that all of his sexual tensions were mounting, asserting themselves like never before. He moved closer, pressing his tall, muscular body against Shad's smaller one.

Shad's trembling increased, though he made no move to escape from Jaeger's hold. Jaeger wrapped his fingers in the boy's hair and pulled the youth's head back, exposing his neck. A tiny voice screamed in Jaeger's mind, pleading with him to stop. But it was too late; he had gone too far. There was no turning back.

With one swift movement, Jaeger lowered his head and bit into the boy's skin. Warm blood flowed into his mouth, sent his senses soaring. He sucked at it hungrily, like a man too long without water. Each mouthful brought him closer and closer to the pinnacle of delight; and when he finally reached it, his entire body convulsed with relief.

Shad went limp, sliding down the wall to land in a heap on the hay. Jaeger leaned his forehead against the wall, too overwhelmed with this new emotion to do much else. For a moment, he did not move.

Then, overpowering guilt tore through him, ravaged his heart and soul. His gaze shot to Shad, and he crouched beside the boy. Quickly, he felt for a pulse. A hiss of relief escaped him when he found it. The boy was still alive.

Jaeger whirled as the other youth groaned and stirred in the hay. Panic-stricken, Jaeger leaped up and bolted from the stall. His pace was fast and furious, and he did not wait until he was clear of the barn before allowing himself to shapeshift into one of his animal forms, a raven. He shot into the night sky, winging his way over the village, turning toward the lake beyond. He would fly; fly forever, out over that vast expanse of water. When he tired, he would fall, to drown in the lake's murky depths and take with him the horrible guilt of what he had just done.

Chapter Four

"Jaeger?"

The soft voice startled Jaeger to his feet. He whirled to see Rhiannon stepping carefully over the slippery rocks toward him. How? How could she know it was him? He had assumed the Illusion of an aged man, as weathered and bent as the crumbling wooden docks beside him. He was speechless as she approached him.

"I was worried about you," she said quietly, stopping within arm's reach. "When you didn't return last eve, I thought something horrible had happened. I don't trust the people in this village anymore. Are you all right?"

Jaeger swallowed hard, finally finding his voice. "I'm fine," he mumbled, "but you must have mistaken me for someone else."

A smile crossed her full lips and her blue gaze settled on his. "No mistake. Auras don't lie."

"Auras?"

"The light surrounding you, revealing who and what you truly are."

"What I am?"

Rhiannon sighed and placed her hand on his arm, then gasped and quickly drew back. What little color was in her cheeks faded. Jaeger took a step back as well. Obviously, she had finally realized just what he was, and it both frightened and repulsed her. He turned away.

"Go, Rhiannon," he whispered. "Go away. It's not safe for you with me. Not now."

"You were going to kill yourself," she said softly, astonishment in her voice. "Why?"

Jaeger turned back to face her, stunned. "H...how did you know that?"

It was Rhiannon's turn to avert her gaze. "When I touched you, I...I felt the pain and heartache. Your lights told me what you did not."

He studied her for a long moment, then sat down on a chunk of driftwood. "Did they also tell you why I wanted to kill myself?"

"They didn't have to. The story is all over the village." She sat down beside him. "The boy, Shad, will live. He doesn't remember much; only that he was attacked by a Vector. He doesn't remember the man's face, of course."

Jaeger sat very still, amazed at the ease with which Rhiannon spoke of his kind, of what he had done, of who he was. He was even more amazed when she reached out and took his cold hand in her warm one. He brought his gaze to meet hers.

"If you know what I am, why haven't you turned me over to the constable?" He could scarcely get the words out.

"Why would I do that, Jaeger? You have no more control over what you are than I do."

"You?"

She nodded, her dark hair tumbling about her shoulders. She drew her cloak tighter. Jaeger recognized it as one of his; and, for some reason, the thought of her snuggled in its warmth brought him warmth as well, but of a different kind. He waited for her to answer his query, but it seemed she would remain silent. He sighed and looked out over the water before him. His astonishment slowly faded, replaced by resignation.

"I don't understand it, Rhiannon," he said quietly. "I had never taken human blood before, and now I've become a monster. That's why you must leave me. That's why it is no longer safe for you to be in my company. I...I don't know that I can control my desires any longer, and I don't want to hurt you."

She laughed softly, the sound sending a tingle down Jaeger's spine. Her grip tightened about his hand. "You won't hurt me, Jaeger. I know that. I do not fear you at all."

Jaeger looked at her. He knew what it was now. It was the hypnosis. It was how the Vector controlled his victim. The way he had controlled Shad so that the boy had not called out for help or run from him. Was he now controlling Rhiannon the same way? If so, he didn't want to, yet he didn't know how to stop it. He pulled his hand away from hers and rose.

"You don't know what you're saying," he told her. "You need to go home, back where you belong. Surely your family is agonizing over your absence."

"I don't think so," she said. "They're the reason I'm here."

"Why?" Jaeger asked without thinking. He flushed. "That was rude. I didn't mean to pry."

"You didn't." She rose, but offered no further explanation. "Come back to the inn with me. Please. You need to rest. And the sun will be up soon."

Jaeger looked at the lightening skies. "The sun? It has never bothered me before. Why would it now?"

"Because now you are...different," she said, tugging gently on his arm. "Come."

Jaeger looked from the sky to her face, losing himself once again in the blue depths of her eyes. They seemed to change intensity. That first moment she had awakened, they had been a limpid, crystal blue, as if they would fade to clear at any moment. Now they were the deepest blue-green, like a glacial pool of water. He frowned, puzzled, but allowed her to lead him toward the inn.

They reached it just as the sun broke the horizon. It hit Jaeger on the side of his face, and he gasped as unexpected pain shot through him. He reached up to clutch at his cheek even as Rhiannon pulled him into the safety of shadows blanketing the back alleyway.

"Let's get upstairs," she urged.

Reeling, Jaeger followed her lead, stumbling up the narrow servant's stair and down the empty hallway to his room. Rhiannon pulled the key from her pocket, opened the door, and led him inside.

"Sit down," she ordered and hurried toward a large basket sitting on the side table.

"What's that?" Jaeger asked, shutting and bolting the door behind him. He staggered to a chair and collapsed into it, fanning his burning skin with one hand.

"I went out to the market after you left last eve. I wanted to get a few things. Fortunately, aloe was one of them. Here." She returned to him with a small vial full of clear liquid.

"What is it for?"

"Burns," she replied quietly and pulled his hand from his cheek. She gently applied the cool gel, bringing instant relief to the stinging pain he had been experiencing.

"Burns?" he murmured, then rose and started toward the mirror.

"No!" Rhiannon stopped him. "No, Jaeger, don't."

He frowned at her and continued toward the mirror. Terror ran through him as he stood before it. He could not see his reflection. He could see Rhiannon standing behind him, her eyes sparkling with tears, but he could not see himself.

Chapter Five

J aeger pulled his blanket tighter around him and stared morosely into the flames. Rhiannon had covered all of the windows with blankets, bringing night to the daytime. He hated it. Hated shutting out the sun, hated being relegated to slinking about in the dark of night. Yet, he could not deny the burn that still brought tears of pain to his eyes, a burn caused by his brief encounter with the sun. He shivered and hunched further into his chair.

"Please, Jaeger," Rhiannon said softly. "Have some soup. You're chilled through."

He sighed and glanced toward her. Though the only light in the room came from the fire, he could see her quite clearly. She was perched on the end of the bed, watching him. The firelight flickered off her creamy skin, danced in her blue eyes, created interesting shadows in her long, dark tresses.

She had bathed earlier and wore one of his tunics. Since he was so much taller, it fit her like a shift, hitting her at mid-thigh. Slender, white legs lay against the bed's dark coverlets, enticing Jaeger closer. It was an enticement he was resisting, though it wasn't easy. He wanted her. He wanted to hold her, caress her, and feel her body against his. He wanted to experience that rush of sensuality he had experienced with Shad and knew that, with Rhiannon, it would be physical as well as mental. He shuddered again and looked back at the fire. He wished she would go; yet he knew he couldn't bear it if she did.

He heard her rise and move toward him. He steeled himself against her closeness but nearly lost his resolve when she settled on the floor beside his feet. She held up a steaming mug of soup, a hopeful smile on her lips. Jaeger sighed and took the offering.

After he had managed a few sips, she leaned forward, resting her chin on an arm she draped across his knees.

"Tell me why, Jaeger," she said softly.

At once, he knew to what she referred. "Because I'm a coward. I couldn't kill myself. I tried, but I just couldn't do it."

"A coward?" Rhiannon laughed at that. "How old are you, Jaeger?"

The question surprised him. He shrugged and took another sip of the soup. "I don't know. In human years, maybe one hundred or more. In Vector years, only about twenty. Why?"

"So, for all of those years, you never took human blood?" she asked.

"No. I didn't. I made a vow to my mother on her deathbed. I have abided by that vow." He paused. "Until now."

"That must have taken a lot of willpower and courage. A hundred years is a long time."

Again, he shrugged, not understanding what she was getting at.

She smiled up at him. "Don't you see how little coward there is in you? You could have been like all the other Vectors. You could have taken your first blood at an early age and kept on. Instead, you chose to isolate yourself from your own kind, to go against your heritage. You could have taken me when you found me. You didn't. You helped me. How many other Vectors would have done the same?"

He stared at her in astonishment. Her words drifted into his heart, edged out the self-recrimination he had harbored there ever since turning his raven form back toward land. He had known even as he had flown that he would not be able to simply plunge into the dark ocean, to let it swallow him, to end his life. He had returned to the beach, assumed the form of the old man, and sat the entire night, ignoring the misty rain and the chill creeping through him.

Jaeger had never expected Rhiannon to look for him. Had certainly never dreamed she would rescue him as she had. And could never have believed she would accept him for who and what he was. Yet, here she sat, looking up at him with caring and devotion evident in her blue eyes.

"Are you sure I am not--" he started.

She shushed him with a gentle squeeze on his leg. "You are not controlling me in any way, Jaeger. I assure you of that."

He was not convinced but said nothing more about it. He took another sip of his soup, realizing it was beginning to take the chill from his insides.

"I shall have to leave this village soon," he said, wondering what her response would be.

"I thought as much." She paused, chewing on her lip. "I would like to come with you, if you will have me."

The words stunned Jaeger. A soft gasp of disbelief escaped him unbidden. "Why?" he breathed.

"Why?" For a moment, she merely studied him, then she turned and faced the fire, leaning her back against his legs.

Her dark hair lay on his knees; and, without thinking, he reached out to run his fingers through its softness.

Rhiannon let out a sigh of contentment. "We need each other, Jaeger. I knew that the moment I opened my eyes and saw you."

"You knew? About me? About Vectors? From the first?"

She nodded. "But it didn't frighten me. I knew I could trust you, Jaeger. Your colors are those of a kind and decent man."

He snorted. "Kind and decent? Hardly. I now steal people's lives to support my own. That's hardly kind and decent."

She twisted to face him, coming to her knees. "You have never killed a human, Jaeger. Can all your Vector friends claim the same?"

Jaeger hesitated, his thoughts on Celd and the barmaid. He wondered if the girl was still alive, and, if so, in what condition.

"She's not," Rhiannon said quietly.

Jaeger started. "What? H-how did you know what I was thinking? What do you mean she's not? She's dead?"

Rhiannon nodded solemnly. "I'm sorry. I heard the news when I was in the market last eve."

Jaeger set his cup down and covered his face with both hands. He couldn't stop the tears that burned his eyes, brought a lump to his throat. He could have prevented it. He could have done something to stop Celd. He should have.

"No," Rhiannon said. "You couldn't have stopped him. Besides, she wouldn't have listened to you. You know that. She was under his spell."

"As you are under mine," Jaeger sobbed. "Please, Rhiannon, you need to go. Leave me. Leave, before I hurt you. Before I...kill you."

She took his hands, pulled them away from his face, and looked into his eyes. "You will not kill me."

"How do you know that?" He tipped his head back to stare at the ceiling, at the grotesque shadows created by the dancing flames. "I almost killed Shad. And do you know why?"

"Yes," she answered before he could go on.

He turned his gaze back on her. "Do you really?"

"Yes," she said again. "Because you are coming into your manhood now. The blood calls to you, lures you."

Jaeger stared at her, completely dumbfounded. "How do you know of me? Of my kind? Who are you?"

Rhiannon was quiet a moment, then she leaned forward and brushed her lips across his. He started at the touch, though his heart leapt in his chest. She smiled, put one hand at the back of his neck, and once again pressed her lips against his. This time, Jaeger kissed her back.

It was delicious, more so than anything he had ever experienced. He lifted his hands and tangled his fingers in her hair, holding her face close so that he might kiss her long and hard. She tasted sweet, fresh, and young. He drew back, panting, then sucked in his breath as she began to kiss his face with light, feathery touches. Even when she kissed his burned cheek, it brought him only delight. He closed his eyes, sinking further into the bliss she provided.

Her hands moved against his chest, and he felt her unlace his tunic. He shuddered when her smooth, soft hands caressed his skin beneath the fabric. His body was responding with alarming speed and intensity. He took a deep breath and gripped her arms, pushing her away.

"You don't know what you're doing," he managed, though his breathing was hard and fast.

"Yes, I do, Jaeger. I do." Her hands moved to his waist, her fingers easing open the ties to his breeches.

"Please, Rhiannon," he begged, "this is new to me. What if I can't...I can't stop. I don't want to hurt you."

"I told you, Jaeger. You won't hurt me. I trust you." She tilted her head at him. "Don't you want to be with me, Jaeger?"

"Oh, by the sands of time! I do, Rhiannon."

"Then, be with me." She stood and with one smooth movement peeled off the tunic she wore and dropped it to the floor.

Jaeger's mouth gaped open and he attempted to avert his gaze, but couldn't. The firelight backlit her body, making it appear to glow. He drank in every lovely curve, every twist of her sensuous body. It was more than he could stand.

He surged to his feet, intent on escaping this torment, sure that he would end up doing something horrible. Instead, his breeches slid down to his knees. He stumbled, grabbing at the chair to stop his fall. Embarrassment tore through him as Rhiannon took his arm. Her touch ignited a new fire within him, and he moaned helplessly. She turned him to face her.

Where he expected to see ridicule, he saw only desire. She smiled and hugged him gently, then kissed him again, standing on tiptoe to do so. Gently, without hesitation, she led him to the bed. And, not once did Jaeger think about the blood that ran through Rhiannon's veins.

He woke hours later. The room was dark, warm...and empty. He sat up, his gaze searching the shadows for any sign of Rhiannon. She was gone. A stab of grief went through Jaeger's heart. Grief and self-reproachment. What had he done? To make use of her like that. He had never done this before. Never been with a woman in that way. For a long moment, he sat, staring at the remains of the fire. She was gone. Well, why should she stay? She had no reason to. She was probably disgusted with him. Yet, she had been the one to lead him to the bed, to strip off both her clothes and his. It had been her decision. Or had it? Had he unknowingly hypnotized her? He shook his head. He needed to stop coming to that conclusion. Perhaps she had done what she had done simply because she had wanted to. Jaeger knew there were women out there like that. They enjoyed sex, seduced men, but there was no longevity in the relationship. It was over. He had to accept that.

He shook his head, feeling like a fool, and climbed to his feet. He snatched up his robe and wrapped it around himself before going to the window. Traces of daylight seeped around the heavy blanket Rhiannon had placed over the window. After a moment's hesitation, Jaeger pulled back one edge to peer out into the streets.

Pain immediately flooded his eyes; and he gasped, backing away from the window. He rubbed at his face as tears streamed down his cheeks, tears that were caused by more than the bright daylight beyond his room. He slouched into his chair, unable to stop the sobs that wracked his body.

He cried for the loss of his mother and father, for the loss of Rhiannon and for the loss of who he had once been. He hated this new life, hated everything about it. And he hated himself for not being able to bring it to a close. He lifted his head, his gaze settling on the blanketed window. What would happen if he strode into the street? If he walked out into the full afternoon sunshine? Would he simply crumple and die, there in the streets? Would he burst into flame for all to witness?

The opening of the door startled him. He leapt to his feet, whirling. Rhiannon entered, carrying a large basket filled with fresh fruits and herbs. There was a blush on her pale cheeks and a smile on her lips that faded when she saw Jaeger.

"What's wrong?" she cried, setting her basket on the side table.

"Nothing!" he retorted, with more anger than he had intended. He turned and threw himself back into the chair.

A moment later, he felt Rhiannon's hands on his shoulders, rubbing gently. Though he tried to remain stiff and unaccepting, he found he could not. Her touch only brought out more tears.

"Jaeger?" She came around to face him. She placed one finger under his chin and lifted his head. "Your eyes!" she gasped. "What did you do?"

"Nothing," he mumbled, though they still stung and teared.

Rhiannon glanced toward the window, then back at Jaeger. He sighed.

"I just wondered where you were, that's all," he said softly.

"Oh, Jaeger, I'm sorry. I didn't want to wake you." She leaned forward and kissed his forehead.

"You could have left a note," he whispered, realizing how childish he sounded.

She smiled. "I don't know how to write."

He looked at her, saw the sincerity in the blue eyes, and his doubts vanished. He reached up and drew her onto his lap, hugging her to him. Only now was he aware that he was trembling. Rhiannon must have noticed as well, for she wrapped her arms around him and held him tight.

"I won't leave you, Jaeger," she whispered. "Not now. Not ever."

He frowned. "You barely know me. How can you make such a statement?"

"I just can," she replied, then pushed away from him. "I brought you some dinner. I think I have something here for your eyes as well. And the fire could use more wood."

He watched her move toward the basket of food, puzzled by her words and actions. Slowly, he rose, threw several chunks of wood on the fire, then approached her. She was busy laying out the fruit she had brought, but stopped when Jaeger touched her arm. He turned her to face him.

"Who are you?" he asked, this time determined to get an answer. "How can you know my thoughts, my desires? How can you claim a piece of my heart and yet show no fear at what I am?"

She studied his face for a moment, then reached up and placed one soft palm against his cheek. He claimed her hand and kissed it gently, still waiting for an answer. Finally, it came, though it answered nothing.

"I am your savior, Jaeger. Just as you are mine. Over time, you will see what I mean. The stage has been set, Jaeger. It will be a new life for both of us. I promise you that." She stood on tiptoe and kissed him lightly. "I promise you that."

Jaeger gazed into her eyes and hugged her. So what if her answer was cryptic. She felt right in his arms. He kissed the top of her head, then nuzzled into her soft hair. Rhiannon giggled, worked her hands beneath his robe, and slid it from his shoulders. Her mouth moved gently, softly over his exposed flesh, sending shivers of anticipation through him. And again, he fell under her spell.

Jaeger woke to hard pounding on his door. He staggered from the bed, rubbing at his face. Rhiannon pulled the blankets close, her eyes wide with alarm.

"Who is it?" Jaeger called through the heavy wooden door.

"Open up, Jaeg! It's Celd!"

"Celd," Jaeger breathed. His gaze shot to Rhiannon. "You must hide. Quickly."

He was surprised when she made no argument. She wrapped a blanket about her and slipped into the large armoire that stood against one wall. Jaeger snatched up his robe, pulled it on, and let Celd into the room.

The Vector staggered past him. His face was flushed as if he had been running some distance, but he wore a wide, pleased smile. He collapsed into the chair before the hearth.

"What are you doing here?" Jaeger asked, unable to hold back the contempt in his voice.

Celd raised one eyebrow at him. "You must have heard about the barmaid, judging from your tone."

"Yes, I did."

"And, as usual, you don't approve." Celd shook his head, draping one long leg over the arm of the chair. "Tell me, Jaeger, what's the difference between that and taking the life of some poor animal for food? How many goats have you bled to death in your lifetime?"

"Very few," Jaeger said, lowering his voice. He eyed Celd with growing impatience. "Is there something I can do for you?"

"No, not really. I just came here to tell you the news."

"News?"

"Yes. Do you remember we were discussing the Sovereign's Chosen?"

Jaeger nodded, his brow furrowing. Celd grinned at him and thumped his own chest.

"Me! The Sovereign has made me a Chosen. Can you believe that?"

In fact, Jaeger could. He had always suspected that Celd had an influential place with the Sovereign. The announcement of his appointment came as no surprise, only an irritant. The arrogant Vector was already full of pride. Now, he would be insufferable.

"Well, then," Jaeger said, moving toward the side table for a glass of wine, "I guess congratulations are in order. I'm pleased for you. I suppose this means you'll be returning to the Lair to receive the embryo?"

Celd shook his head and patted his groin. "Already done, my friend."

Jaeger looked at him in surprise. "Done? Here? How?"

Celd laughed. "I can't tell you that, Jaeg. Privileged information."

"I see." Jaeger handed the full wineglass to Celd. "I would suppose, then, that you'll begin looking for a hostess?"

"Yes, and that's where I want your help, Jaeg," Celd said sitting up straighter.

Jaeger started. "My help?"

Celd nodded. "Remember how I said I was on the trail of a Bleeder? Well, I lost her, but I think she's close by. I want you to help me find her."

Jaeger turned back to the side table, hoping Celd didn't sense his panic and rage. He poured another glass of wine, trying to calm his nerves and temper. "How can I help you? Unless she's part goat, I really don't have a sense for these things." He hoped his attempt at humor would distract Celd.

The Vector laughed. "Not true, my friend. Oh, don't try to deny it. It was you who near drained that boy in the stables. Although why you left him alive, I don't know. Not very smart, Jaeg."

Jaeger took a long drink of his wine. It burned a path to his stomach, where it settled like a flaming torch. "I took what I needed. I saw no reason to do more than that."

"People are talking, Jaeg. First the child, then the barmaid, now the boy. Tensions are rising in this little village."

Jaeger stiffened. "Then I suggest it might be time for you to move on, Celd."

"I agree," the Vector said. "But not before I find the Bleeder."

"Why do you want her so badly?"

"Because, Jaeg," Celd said getting to his feet, "I have plans to make her my hostess."

Jaeger reeled as surely as if he'd been delivered a blow to the gut. He gripped the edge of the side table as Celd studied him through narrowed eyes.

"You don't look so good, Jaeg," Celd said, swaggering toward him. He reached out with his free hand and turned Jaeger's face toward him.

"You've been out in the sun. Not a good idea. But you're learning." He gestured at the blanket-covered windows.

Jaeger sagged into the nearest chair. "I'm tired, Celd. Can we finish this discussion later?"

"You need to feed, Jaeger," Celd said, hunkering down in front of him.

"No!" Jaeger cried. "I just did! I mean, the boy...he..."

"He wasn't enough, Jaeger. You'll need to feed more often until your system gets used to this new food source."

"Gets used to it?" Jaeger eyed him.

Celd straightened and drained the wine from his glass. "Yes. It's a big adjustment from goat's blood. And it's a big adjustment to the needs of your Growth. Your body requires what human blood can give you now. Which is exactly why Vectors are born to human hostesses. There's something in human blood that keeps us strong. I'm sure even you've noticed it by now. Though exactly how you'll be affected is a mystery. It will be interesting to see how you react to your Growth."

Jaeger tensed. Celd never failed to get in a barb about his halfling state. Yet, Jaeger had been wondering the same. So far, his reactions to his Growth had seemed fairly profound. At least to him.

"Still," Celd continued, seemingly oblivious to his silence, "you should find that your reactions to light and the need to feed will diminish with time. That is, if you feed adequately. And I don't mean on goat's blood."

Jaeger moaned in despair. "And if I don't take in human blood?"

Celd shrugged. "Well, if you have enough Vector in you, you'll wither and die, Jaeg. It's a horrible death, full of pain. Each part of the body shuts down, slowly, in agony." He shuddered and set his empty glass on the table. "I've seen it only once, as punishment, and believe me, Jaeger, you don't want to go like that."

"And if I don't want to live like this?" Jaeger motioned at the dark room.

Again, Celd shrugged. "It's your choice, Jaeg." He moved to the window and peered outside into evening light.

Jaeger watched him. "When you arrived, you looked as if you had been running. Is there something wrong?"

"Oh, nothing to worry over. Some old farmer caught me in the stable with his daughter. I gave him a run for it."

Rage tore through Jaeger. "And you came here? You led them here?"

"Relax, Jaeg. I shapeshifted. That old man and his boys are probably still crashing around in the woods looking for me. Hell, by now he's probably lying back in the road, dead from heart failure." The thought seemed to intrigue Celd, and he moved toward the door. "Think I'll go have a check. His daughter was good, but she was awfully small."

"Get out of here," Jaeger seethed.

Celd slowly turned, his face suddenly cold. "Watch your words, Jaeger. I've been tolerant of you and your attitude for too many years. Please remember who I am, and afford me the respect I deserve."

Jaeger drew back, well aware of Celd's new position. Now that he was one of the Chosen, another Vector could be severely punished at just a word from him. Perhaps even made to suffer the horrible death Celd had described.

"I apologize, Celd," Jaeger said, trying to sound contrite. "My only excuse is my illness."

Celd studied him for a moment, then abruptly smiled and clapped him on the shoulder.

"I understand, Jaeg. Believe me, I do. But you shouldn't think of it as an illness. It's simply part of who you are. Embrace it with joy." He turned back toward the door, then stopped, his face thoughtful. "Oh, and if you see that Bleeder, you will tell me, won't you?"

Jaeger tipped his head in acknowledgment, his heart aching. Celd smiled and left. Jaeger immediately locked the door, then leaned against it in despair. What could he do? How could he go against one of the Chosen? He glanced toward the armoire, then slowly went to it. He touched the metal handle, then jerked backward in alarm. It had given him a jarring shock. Startled, he appraised his hand for a burn and found none. Still, the tingly sensation crawled up his arm like a snake twisting about his nerves.

"Rhiannon?" he whispered, shaking his hand. "He's gone."

The door swung open, though Jaeger had not seen the handle turn. He frowned in confusion. Rhiannon was crouched in the corner of the armoire, clutching the blanket to her bosom. Even in the dim light, Jaeger could see she was pale, her eyes half-lidded, as if with exhaustion. He reached for her, but she shook her head.

"Wait," she murmured, closing her eyes. It was several moments before she opened them again, and they were glassy with fatigue. "Now," she whispered.

Confused, Jaeger took her hand and helped her from the cupboard, then caught her as she collapsed. Alarmed, he picked her up and placed her gently on the bed.

"What is it?" he asked softly, brushing her dark hair from her face. "What's wrong? Could you not breathe in there? I shouldn't have allowed Celd to stay so long. I should have told him to leave at the first. I shouldn't even have let him in!"

Rhiannon quieted him with one small finger to his lips. "It's not lack of air, Jaeger," she told him. "I just need to rest. I'll be fine. Lay beside me. Keep me warm."

Jaeger slid into the blankets beside her and pulled her into his arms. She was shivering, her skin cool to the touch. It only increased his panic. He rose and placed more wood on the fire, then fetched another blanket from the settee and covered Rhiannon before once more lying beside her.

"Tell me what's wrong. What can I do to help you?"

She gave a small smile and kissed him gently on the cheek. "You can feed on me," she whispered.

He drew back with a gasp. "No! I would never do that, Rhiannon."

"You must," she said. "You know that I am a Bleeder. Use your Vector senses, Jaeger."

He stared at her in confusion and uncertainty. Then, slowly, he became aware of the scent of iron. It rose into the air, hovered, then descended on him like a wet, heavy fog. It pressed against his skin, seeped into his pores, settled into his mind. It aroused him with a need that had nothing to do with sex, yet fueled his desire nonetheless. Frightened by the intensity of the sensation, he relaxed his hold on Rhiannon. She sighed and pulled him back.

"No," he said again, though his willpower was faltering. "No, Rhiannon, please don't ask this. I can't take you, I won't." He climbed from the bed, shaking, forcing his desires back. He was sure that once he began to feed on Rhiannon, he wouldn't be able to stop, that he would drain her completely in his wild lust, in his need for satiation. The very idea sent terror to his gut.

She nodded, though resignation lay heavy in her blue eyes. "I understand."

"Do you? Do you really? Do you understand that I might not be able to stop? This is all so new to me, Rhiannon. I...I almost killed that boy in the stables. I might have, had not his companion wakened." He paced to the fire and leaned one hand against the mantle. "I can't take the risk, not with you."

"Even if it means saving my life?"

He looked at her, puzzled. "What do you mean?"

"What do you know of Bleeders, Jaeger?"

He shrugged. "Not a lot. Only that they exist. They seem to have a way of regenerating their blood supply faster than most humans, from what I understand."

"That is the way of some," she agreed. "Basically, they have too much blood and must be bled at regular times to keep from drowning in it. But there are other kinds of Bleeders as well."

"Others?" Jaeger shook his head. He was having a hard time concentrating on her words. The scent of iron was growing stronger, more enticing. His gaze drifted to her neck, and he rapidly forced it away.

"Yes. I am an iron Bleeder, for lack of a better term. I produce too much iron in my blood. The only way to get rid of it is to be bled."

He frowned, clutching the mantle tighter, determined to keep his distance from her. "And how do you know this?"

She smiled, though there was much sadness in it. "Because of what I am, Jaeger." She rose, shedding her blankets.

Jaeger drew a quick breath as the firelight played off her creamy white skin. She approached him with catlike movements, setting his heart racing. His gaze went to her throat and stayed there.

"And what are you?" he rasped as she stopped directly in front of him.

She tilted her head back to look into his eyes. Her dark hair slid from her shoulders, baring her neck. Her artery pulsed, throbbing with each heartbeat, matching his own. Without conscious thought, he took her into his arms, closing his eyes, inhaling the intoxicating smell of iron. His mouth caressed her skin, tasting, touching. His tongue flicked out and drew a small, wet circle on her pulse. She let out a soft gasp and arched back in his arms. A heady rush of iron surrounded Jaeger, consumed him, drove him.

He tightened his grip on her, tangled one hand in her long tresses while he slid the other down her hips, and lifted her. Rhiannon wrapped her legs about his waist, her arms around his shoulders. The feel of her skin, reeking with the metallic scent of her blood against his was more than Jaeger could bear. She let out no more than a soft cry as his incisors pierced her flesh.

The first taste of her blood sent Jaeger's senses spinning. He drew more, dizzy with his need, his wants, his desires. She moaned and writhed in his arms. The movement, her taste, her sounds, pushed Jaeger to ecstasy. He took one last mouthful, and then threw back his head, ecstasy claiming him.

Rhiannon clung to him, her breathing hard and fast, her body limp. Jaeger stumbled to the bed, where he laid her down gently, and covered her. For long moments, neither of them moved nor spoke. Then Rhiannon smiled, her eyes already half closed.

"I'm a witch, Jaeger," she mumbled. "A witch."

Chapter Seven

Jaeger sat on the edge of the bed, his gaze on Rhiannon. She slept now, the peaceful, innocent sleep of the satiated. Two, small bite marks stood out on her neck like tiny red beacons. Jaeger reached out and touched them gently, then drew back as she stirred. She opened her eyes and gave him a languid smile.

"Good eve," she murmured.

"Good eve," he returned softly. "It's time to leave. I've got everything packed."

"Must we go tonight?" she protested, her voice weak.

"Yes." He pulled her from the bed, trying to ignore her nakedness. "I've purchased you some clothing that will fit you far better than--"

"You went out?" she interrupted.

"Yes." He frowned, puzzled by her alarm.

"But the townspeople, they..."

"Don't know me," he finished. "I use two Illusions, neither of them receptive to conversation." He hesitated, handing her the white, linen blouse and brown, wool skirt he had bought. "What do you see when you look at me, Rhiannon? What did you see that first time you opened your eyes on me?"

She smiled, relaxing, her panic fading. "A very handsome and desirable man. A man who sets my heart racing, who brings my sexuality alive."

Jaeger flushed at the words. "Rhiannon," he began, "I want you to know that this is not my usual behavior. I...I mean, I don't usually..." He faltered, gesturing feebly at the bed.

Rhiannon giggled and pressed against him. "Nor do I, Jaeger," she purred. "But I knew the moment I saw you that we belonged together."

He took a deep breath, feeling the sweet warmth of her body next to his. He wanted to make love to her again, to reach that pinnacle of delight with her one more time. Sternly, he chastised himself for his constant lustful thoughts and gently pushed her away.

"We need to leave, Rhiannon," he said softly.

She nodded and began to dress. "And where do we go? You must have shelter before daybreak."

The words stung, and Jaeger involuntarily winced, though he knew them to be true. "There is another village not far from here. We will go there, and from there to another village, and yet another, until we are well away from this place."

Rhiannon tied the blue sash about her waist. Jaeger had bought it for no other reason than that it reminded him of her eyes. She pulled on her boots and eyed him thoughtfully. "And what do we flee?"

Jaeger was surprised at her perception, yet he did not want to tell her the truth. He didn't want to tell her how witches were sought after by

Vectors, to become not only their mates, but their slaves. Now Jaeger understood why Celd's thoughts had centered on Rhiannon, on finding her, on making her the hostess for his child. He intended to take her in mind, body, and spirit. He would completely possess her, forcing her to do his bidding, increasing his strength and power through her use of magic and spells. It was something Jaeger was determined to thwart.

The only way to prevent Celd from having his way with Rhiannon was to run. If Celd came asking for Rhiannon, Jaeger wouldn't be able to deny him. Celd was one of the Chosen now, and with that title came power. It was a position and power far above any that Jaeger could ever hope to hold.

He picked up the pack and slung it over his shoulder, then took Rhiannon's hand and kissed it. "I never stay long in one village. I'm a wanderer, I guess. I've already paid for the room. Let's go down the back way."

She agreed, allowing him to lead her down the narrow staircase and into the dark alley. Jaeger kept to the shadows, moving quickly and quietly, hoping Celd was busy elsewhere. He took a quick whiff of the air around him, noticing the lack of the iron scent. His gaze shifted to Rhiannon. Apparently, when he bled her, he had succeeded in tempering the smell of iron. And if Celd couldn't sense her, he couldn't come after her. Jaeger wondered if she had been aware of this, if that was also why she had been so insistent upon being bled.

They walked in silence until they were well clear of the village; then Jaeger stopped and removed the pack. Rhiannon watched him with obvious curiosity.

"I do not expect you to walk the distance to the next village," he told her. "I will shapeshift."

"I've never seen such," Rhiannon said softly, true awe in her blue eyes.

She picked up the pack and stepped back.

Jaeger took a deep breath, let it out slowly, and allowed himself to shift into a horse. It was a stretch, he knew that, but he was counting on the strength Rhiannon's blood had given him. He wasn't sure how long he could maintain the shape and only hoped it would last until they could get to another village safely.

Rhiannon laughed softly and approached him. She ran one hand along his neck, then looked directly into his dark eyes.

"You make a proud stallion," she whispered. "Can you understand me?"

He bobbed his head up and down. He could understand her quite well, though he would not be able to converse with her until he shifted back. He bent his forelegs to allow her purchase to his back. Once she'd settled, he straightened and turned north.

Rhiannon leaned low over his neck and whispered into his ear, "You know, don't you, that a horse is a very sensual animal?"

Though he was sure it was impossible, Jaeger thought he blushed. With a toss of his head, he broke into a gallop, praying that Celd was nowhere near.

Morning came sooner than Jaeger had expected. As the skies began to lighten, his strength waned, slowing his gait from a gallop to a slow trot and, finally, a walk. Rhiannon pulled against his mane, halting him, and slid from his back.

"That's far enough," she said. "You have to change back."

Jaeger had no energy left to argue. He shifted almost without willing it, and then stumbled and sagged to the ground, exhausted. Rhiannon knelt beside him, wrapped her arms about his shoulders, and gently kissed his cheek.

He glanced toward the horizon where the village lay nestled on a mountain slope. "I'm not going to make it, Rhiannon," he whispered. "I'm too tired to walk, and the sun..."

She frowned, following his gaze. "I have an idea, Jaeger, but I don't know if you can do it."

"I can try," he said.

"I know shifting is draining for you, but if you could shift into something very small, like a mouse, I could put you in my pocket and protect you from the sunlight."

Jaeger stared at her, actually amused by the prospect. He had never done anything such as she was suggesting, but it didn't seem there was any other choice. He didn't relish the thought of having his skin seared by the sun. Still, he wasn't sure if he had enough energy to shapeshift at all, even to something small, let alone hold the shape. He needed blood, but he wasn't about to ask her for it. No, he would take his chances. Besides, the village didn't look that far away. Jaeger glanced again at the rising sun.

"Very well."

It was harder than he expected, his need for blood more pronounced than he had guessed. Rhiannon picked him up gently and held him up to eye level.

"No matter what form you take, Jaeger," she cooed, "you're incredibly handsome." She leaned forward and gave him a light kiss on the nose before tucking him gently into her skirt pocket.

Jaeger settled down in the folds of the cloth, feeling at once protected, yet very vulnerable. Though he possessed great strength and was able to heal from any injury rapidly, he was not immortal. He could be killed if the right weapon were used. In such a small form, it would be an easy task to either impale him with an oak stake or drown him. He doubted that he had the energy to transform back to Vector shape in an emergency. The thought sent his heart pounding, and he prayed that he had, indeed, put his faith in the right person.

She began to walk, and he was soon lulled to sleep by the rhythmic motion. He had no idea how long he had slept when a man's voice woke him. He listened intently as Rhiannon made arrangements for a room, using money from his pack. Filtered light came dimly through the heavy fabric of her skirt, and Jaeger was glad that he had chosen wool. Once in their room, Rhiannon bade him wait a moment while she covered the windows, shutting out the bright sunshine. Only then did she take him out of her pocket. She set him on the wide bed and lay down beside him.

"I know you need blood, Jaeger," she said softly. "Here's a thought. What if you take the blood from me in your present form? It seems that you wouldn't need as much. Maybe just a few drops."

He peered up at her. He had never heard of such a thing before. She held her hand forward, her finger near his mouth.

"Just a few drops, Jaeger," she said again.

Jaeger hesitated, unsure what to do. If he shifted back to his ordinary form, he would need to feed soon. After expending so much energy, he didn't know if he could wait until nightfall. Still, he didn't know if her suggestion would even work. He could be inflicting pain on her to no avail. He didn't want to do that either.

"Please, Jaeger," she whispered. "I shouldn't want you to be trapped in a mouse form." She smiled coyly. "And I shouldn't think you'd want to be."

Jaeger would have chuckled if he could have. Instead, he quickly bit into her finger, drawing blood. She let out a little gasp of pain but did not withdraw her hand. Jaeger drank down the blood almost as fast as it flowed, feeling strength course through his mouse's body. Whether or not that strength would be there when he changed back to Vector form, he didn't know.

When he was satisfied, he drew away and once more shifted. It was surprisingly easy, and he looked at Rhiannon in amazement. "How do you know so much?"

She shrugged, moving into his arms. "It's a gift."

"No," Jaeger murmured, breathing in her essence. "No, Rhiannon, you are the gift. A gift I don't deserve."

"And why not, Jaeger?" she asked, her voice sleepy.

He kept his answer to himself, burying his face in her soft tresses. Yes, she was a rare and beautiful gift. And he was terrified she would be taken from him.

Jaeger held her close, feeling her slip into exhausted slumber. Once he was sure she was asleep, he left her to make a fire. Thoughts tumbled through his weary mind, but they always arrived at the same conclusion.

Jaeger had to leave her.

He had to get her to a safe place where Celd couldn't find her, then he had to leave her. His presence, that mysterious whatever-it-was that drew one Vector to another, would only attract Celd's attention. Just as he had drawn their attention to his mother.

His father had made the decision to take him away from her, for them both to leave her so she could live out her life safe from Vector hands. But he was young. He did not understand why he could never see his beloved mother again. He had pleaded with heart-rending sobs to stay with her. In the face of this, she could not bear to let him go. She had begged his father to stay.

His father could not refuse her even this. Particularly this. It was a decision hastening both their deaths.

And it was all because of him.

His gaze drifted to the bed, and his heart spasmed with grief. How could he leave Rhiannon? He loved her.

The mental pronouncement startled him. He loved her. He didn't want to leave her, didn't want to be without her soft touch, her gentle ministrations, her mysterious wisdom. He straightened, abandoning his attempts at the fire.

He returned to the bed and stood watching her sleep. In all of his years, he had never allowed himself to love, never let down his defenses. When you loved someone, you lost them. It had always been that way for Jaeger.

Death was nothing new to him. He had seen two newborn siblings die hours after their birth, had watched human friends grow old and die, and had witnessed his father's banishment and his mother's murder. It was embedded in his mind's eye, replaying at inopportune times such as this. He wanted to forget it, to erase it from his memory, but he knew he never could. It would stay with him forever, just as the guilt would also stay with him forever.

He sighed, rubbing at his face with both hands. Rhiannon was a human. Humans got old. Humans died. And he would be alone again. The thought drove into his soul, shattered it, and devoured it bit by bit.

How had Rhiannon pierced the shield surrounding his heart? And so easily? Was it only because of his emotional state at the moment, because of what he was going through physically? Was it because she was the first woman with whom he'd made love?

He shook himself. No. There was something more. Something deeper. She had claimed a place in his sheltered heart, had crept in like a thief and stolen his resolve. He loved her, and there was no turning back.

"You fool," he murmured aloud. "Your love will kill her. In the end, it will kill her."

He sagged onto the bed in despair.

Jaeger stopped pacing to glance at the covered window. With agonizing slowness, the sun was setting, bringing night to the village. He had finally managed to get the fire burning, and now it shed its yellow glow over the room. The remains of dinner sat on the table, and Jaeger's gaze flicked over it. He was hungry, but not for food.

"Damn," he cursed quietly. Hard as he tried to suppress his thirst for blood, it called, sending both irritation and excitement through him.

Rhiannon had gone for a bath. If he were going to slip away from her, now would be the time. It was evening. He could shapeshift and be gone. Without a trace, without a word.

No. That wasn't the way to do it. Especially not here. *We're not far enough away from Celd.*

Feeble excuses all. He knew that. And it only served to increase his annoyance with himself. He looked again to the window. It had to be dark enough by now. It had to be. He returned and reached out tentatively to pull aside the blanket.

It was not quite dark outside. Though the light wasn't enough to cause severe pain, it was enough to make his eyes water. He released the blanket just as Rhiannon returned.

"That was wonderful," she sighed.

Jaeger turned, his breath catching in his throat. *By the Sovereign, she was beautiful!*

She had once more slipped into one of his tunics. Her damp hair twisted down her back and shoulders in loose curls. Her face was flushed from the heat of the water she had just left, and the scent of perfumed soap floated across the room, enticing Jaeger closer.

He surrendered, unable to stop himself. He gathered her close, breathing deeply, his hands running over the soft, smooth skin of her bare arms.

She smiled up at him, and stood on tiptoe to kiss his lips. "Go, Jaeger, go relax in a hot bath. It will ease the strain from your muscles."

"Maybe later," he murmured. "I...I have to go out for a bit."

"Why? I'm here."

He drew back, looked into her blue eyes. "No, Rhiannon, not tonight. In fact, I shouldn't have bled you yesterday. It was too soon after your injury. I'm surprised you didn't faint from weakness."

"I know my body, Jaeger. When I use magic, it affects my blood."

He frowned, puzzled, then remembered the sharp jolt he had gotten when he touched the handle of the armoire. He had thought it strange at the time that Celd had not sensed her presence, especially when the scent of iron had been so strong.

"I shielded myself from Celd," she said now, obviously reading his thoughts. "I used magic. In so doing, I increased my iron level. That's why I needed to be bled. That's why I was bleeding when you found me under the dock."

He shook his head, completely confused. Rhiannon opened the pack and took out a brush. She held it out to him and sat down in the chair. Without thinking, he began to brush the tangles from her hair as she talked.

"I had to use magic to escape the men who attacked me. There were four of them. I used far more magic than I should have, and still they got what they sought. I was attempting to bleed myself, to cleanse myself of the iron, but I must have cut too deeply and fainted instead. If you hadn't found me, I likely would have bled to death."

Jaeger started at her words. He hadn't realized how close to death she had been. Or that she had been raped by all four men. Rage boiled through him. What if she was with child? Or diseased? He didn't know how to help her.

Again, she read his concerns. She turned in the chair, getting to her knees on it. "I'm not ill or with child," she assured him. "I knew I couldn't use my magic to stop them, so I used my magic to stop the effects of what they did." She reached up and placed one palm against his cheek. "I'm fine. Really."

Jaeger laid the brush on the table and caught up her hand. "I wish I could find the men who hurt you," he seethed.

"And what? Revenge is not your way, Jaeger."

"For them, I would make an exception."

Rhiannon gave him a weary smile and shook her head. "It is not your way," she said again, her soft voice calming his anger.

He leaned forward and kissed her gently, then straightened. "I must go out, Rhiannon. I will return as quickly as possible."

"Are you sure you won't reconsider?"

"I'm sure. You need time to recover your strength." He paused, stroking her cheek with one finger. "Do you have a family?"

She gave him a quizzical look. "I have my clan. They are all like family to me. Why?"

"Where are they?"

"North of here, last I heard. They rove."

"And why aren't you with them?"

Rhiannon averted her gaze, then abruptly got off the chair. "I--I had things to do. They were going in the wrong direction, that's all."

"Then you can rejoin them at some point?" he asked.

"Yes, at some point."

He was puzzled by the vagueness of her answers. It was as if she didn't want to discuss them at all, and he decided not to pry further. He crossed to the door and took his cloak off the peg.

"I'll be back shortly," he said.

He made his trip brief and purposeful, shapeshifting to a wolf and taking down the first goat he saw. But tonight the blood tasted almost vile, and it was all he could do to gag it down. It gave him some strength, though it was nowhere near as restorative as human blood. After feeding, he shaped himself into a young man and strolled into town.

He went to the pub, the greatest source of gossip in every town, ordered a stein of ale, and sat near the fire. It didn't take him long to pick up on the information being passed about the room. News of the deaths in Skyther had reached this small village as well. Only, now there seemed to have been more than three. Jaeger took a long pull on his ale to wash the fetid taste of animal blood away and tuned an ear to the conversation.

His gut tightened with each word. Five dead now. A farmer and his daughter, both found drained of their blood. Anger burned through Jaeger. Celd's work, no doubt. He thought about the bloodied carcass of the goat he had left in the meadow. He should have taken the time to hide it or bury it. With all of the deaths in Skyther, it was bound to attract more attention than it warranted.

Jaeger drained his stein and rose, then started as a loud crash came from the kitchen.

At once, he was overwhelmed by the smell of fresh blood. He staggered, clutching at the rough-hewn wood table for support. Panicked cries echoed through the air, and a moment later the pub-tender darted into the room. His dark eyes were wide with fear, and he cast a pleading glance over the patrons.

"Anyone!" he cried. "My boy, he's bleeding! Bleeding bad. Someone help! Please!"

There was a general murmuring of sympathy, but no one made a move to assist. The barkeep's gaze fell on Jaeger, the only one standing.

"Can you help, sir? Please? I beg of you. Please?" he cried.

Jaeger started to protest but was stopped by the look of sheer grief on the man's lean face. "I'll try."

"Bless you, sir, bless you. This way! Hurry!"

Jaeger followed him into the kitchen, steeling himself against the scent of blood. A young boy, no more than eight or nine, sat in the center of the floor amidst the shattered remains of crockery, a dazed look on his rapidly paling face. Blood gushed from a gaping wound in his forearm, soaking into his clothing, pooling about his thin legs, and running in a thin rivulet toward a floor drain.

Jaeger snatched up a drying cloth and squatted beside the boy. He wrapped the cloth about the boy's arm, applying pressure as he did so. The child let out a small whimper of pain but did not try to pull away. Jaeger glanced over his shoulder at the barkeep.

"Go to the Hazelwood Inn," he instructed. "Room Two-Twelve. There is a woman there who is learned in healing. Tell her that Jaeger sent for her. Tell her to bring her bag with her."

The barkeep nodded, wiping sweat from his face with his apron. "Will he...will he be all right?"

"I think so," Jaeger replied. "But we need to close up this wound. Is there someplace I can lay him down?"

"Yes, through there. On the cot."

"Good. Now, go, fetch the woman."

The barkeep spun and dashed from the room. Jaeger looked back at the little boy, who was staring up at him without really seeing him. Shock was setting in. Jaeger hoped Rhiannon would be swift.

"Come on, then," Jaeger said softly. Still holding the cloth in place, he scooped up the little boy and carried him into the back room. He placed him gently on the cot and smoothed back sweat-clammy hair from the small, ashen face.

The child gave Jaeger a tiny smile, complete trust in his gray eyes, then fainted. Jaeger sat still, trying to ignore the call of the blood. It had soaked through the cloth and touched the skin of his hand. It was warm, vibrant, alive. He knew it could do more for him, for his strength, than fifty goats. Still, he did not let up on the pressure on the wound. He would not. This boy would not be his. Jaeger closed his eyes and willed Rhiannon to hurry.

As if in response to his unspoken plea, she entered the room, the barkeep one step behind. She cast a swift glance at Jaeger, her gaze both questioning and sympathetic.

"He cut himself on some broken bowls," Jaeger explained, his voice shaking. "The wound is jagged and quite deep. He may have cut the vessel that comes from the heart."

Rhiannon nodded, sitting on the edge of the cot. She opened her bag, took out a container of liquid, and wet a small cloth with it. This she placed beneath the boy's nose and over his mouth. He let out a small moan and went still. Rhiannon looked up at the boy's father.

"It would be best if you busied yourself elsewhere," she told him. "The boy will feel no pain, but your empathy with him will affect you. Go."

The man's gaze went to his son. "He's...he's all I have," he whispered. "Please, don't let him die. Please."

"I'll do my best," Rhiannon said. "But I make no promises."

"I'll go with you," Jaeger said.

"No," Rhiannon countered at once. "I may need your help."

Jaeger grimaced. He didn't want to stay here, to be in the same room with this child, this blood that called to him. Yet, he couldn't tell Rhiannon no. He nodded with a sigh. The barkeep hesitated, then leaned over and kissed his son's forehead before hurrying from the room. Rhiannon rose and closed the door behind him.

"All right. First, I will need to find the vessel from the heart. That has to be closed off or the boy will lose too much blood." She began removing supplies from her bag, some Jaeger recognized, others he had never seen before.

There was a spool of fine thread, a very fine needle, some herbs, and a strange looking bit of metalwork resembling scissors but lacking the cutting edge. She took the glass chimney off the lamp and passed the tool through the flame, then looked up at Jaeger.

"All right, I want you to release the cloth about the wound. After I isolate the bleeding vessel we'll wash the injury and close it."

Jaeger did as she asked. At once, the blood began to pump furiously from the boy's arm, spraying onto Jaeger's hand. He sucked in his breath, closed his eyes, and forced his desires aside.

"There it is," Rhiannon said softly. "It's not an artery, but it's good sized vein. And...I've got it."

Jaeger opened his eyes to see that she had clamped the metal tool about the gushing vein. The blood flow stopped. He watched in fascination as Rhiannon sprinkled a white powder over the entire injury, then held her hand inches above it. She closed her eyes, mumbled a few quiet words, and moved her hand in a circular motion over the wound.

The tissue seemed to shrivel upon itself, like leaves recoiling from a flame. Rhiannon opened her eyes, gave a small smile of satisfaction and unclamped the metal tool. She rose, fetched a pan of water, and gently cleansed the wound.

Jaeger watched in awe and growing pride as she began to sew the wound closed. Each stitch was meticulously done and tied off. When she was finished, a neat row of knots traced up the boy's arm. Rhiannon used the remaining water to clean the blood from the skin, then dried it gently. A clear ointment followed, smeared lightly over the knots. Finally, Rhiannon removed the cloth from the boy's face and sat back with a contented sigh.

"There," she said. "That is all I can do. The rest will be up to the boy and his father."

The boy stirred, letting out a small whimper of pain, and his eyes fluttered open. He stared up at Jaeger and Rhiannon in confusion and alarm. Rhiannon smiled at him in reassurance.

"Fetch his father," she told Jaeger, then stopped him as he rose. "Wash first."

Jaeger looked down at his hands. They were covered with dried blood. Blood he had been able to resist. Perhaps it was as Celd said--he would get used to this need. He quickly washed and went for the barkeep.

The man was huddled at a table, surrounded by sympathetic friends. He looked up at Jaeger, his eyes questioning.

Jaeger smiled. "He is awake. Come."

The little boy looked up as his father entered the room, and broke into tears. "Papa," he sobbed. "I'm sorry I broke the bowls. I'm sorry."

The barkeep fell on his knees beside the bed, gently embracing his son. "Don't worry over the bowls, boy. You're far more precious than some bits of crockery."

"The wound will have to be kept dry and clean," Rhiannon said. "I will leave you this powder. Sprinkle it over the wound for the next few days. The stitches can be removed in seven days' time. After that, he must take care for another week or so. I will also leave you something for his pain. Be sure to give him plenty of water to drink. He needs to make up for the lost blood."

The barkeep nodded, then abruptly grasped her hand and kissed the back of it. "My thanks, gentlewoman! And to you as well, kind sir. I have no money to speak of, but what I have is yours."

"We need no money from you," Jaeger said at once. "Our payment is your thanks." He extended his hand to Rhiannon, who stood up unsteadily.

"Then," the barkeep said. "Allow me to at least make your meals here free of charge."

Jaeger was eager to be away. He could once more smell the iron radiating from Rhiannon's body; see the pallor on her face. She had used magic here, again more than she should have in her state of weakness. He nodded to the barkeep and led Rhiannon from the pub.

It was a short walk to the inn, but halfway up the stairs Rhiannon sagged against him, her face ashen and beaded with sweat. He picked her up and carried her the rest of the way to the room. Once there, he shut and bolted the door, laid her upon the bed and fed.

ours later, Jaeger was jolted awake by a frantic pounding on the door. He stumbled from the bed and staggered across the room to answer. The barkeep was in the hallway, his face pale, his eyes distraught. Jaeger's first thought was of the boy.

"What's happened?" he asked. "Your son--"

"No!" the man interrupted hastily. "Not my boy. It's you. You and the girl. You have to leave. At once!"

"What? Why?"

"Jaeger?" Rhiannon's sleepy voice drifted across the room.

"There's no time for a long explanation," the barkeep said, glancing nervously over his shoulder. "She's a witch. There are some folks here who don't take kindly to her ways. Now, please, get your things together. I have horses waiting for you."

Jaeger was stunned by the man's words. A low rumble came from outside the inn. He saw Rhiannon dart from the bed to the window. She looked back at him, her blue eyes wide.

"They're coming, Jaeger," she whispered.

"God almighty!" the barkeep cried. "I can't let them see me. The horses are out back. I have to go!" He turned and bolted down the hallway.

Jaeger turned to Rhiannon, who was stuffing their personal items into the pack as fast she could.

"Why?" he asked. "Why would they want to hurt you? You saved the boy's life."

"Yes, and used magic to do it," she replied tightly. "Hurry, Jaeger, help me."

He quickly complied, and in moments they were packed and ready to go.

Rhiannon took another look through the window. "They've stopped out front. I think they're trying to decide which room we're in."

Jaeger took a deep breath. "Then, come on. I know the back way out. Let's hope the barkeep was true to his word, and there are horses waiting."

He took her hand and led her into the dimly lit hallway. From there, it was a short walk to the servant's staircase and down to the alley. As promised, two sturdy horses stood waiting. Jaeger lifted up Rhiannon, but before he could mount, a small band of men appeared at the alley's end. They carried torches. Though the light didn't quite reach Jaeger and Rhiannon, it was enough to identify them to the group. And enough for Jaeger to see that the men held a variety of weapons picked up on their way to the inn.

"There she is!" someone shouted. "The witch!"

Something flew past Jaeger's head. He heard Rhiannon cry out in pain and whirled. Her hand was to her cheek, and blood trickled like black ink between her fingers. Rage tore through Jaeger, and before he thought out his actions, he shapeshifted to the most powerful form he could in the confines of the alley--a sleek, steel-muscled black mountain cat.

None of the men had enough light to see the change, and more hard projectiles were thrown. One struck Jaeger on the shoulder, and he let out a roar that echoed between the stone walls of the alley.

The horses immediately shied and bolted. The men scattered as the animals thundered into their midst and past, and then one shouted that he had seen Rhiannon clinging to the back of one of them. Jaeger let out another throaty growl, drawing the group's attention.

"It's her familiar!" a man shouted. "Kill it and you kill her!"

Jaeger wasted no time. He sprang, rage driving his actions. The first man he encountered, the one who had injured Rhiannon, went down with a solid thud. He made only a soft gurgling sound as Jaeger tore open his throat. The other men screamed in terror and backed away, though they all held their weapons ready.

Jaeger spun, blood dripping from his mouth. Blood that was giving him strength, fueling his rage. His gaze shifted from one man to the other, daring any one of them to attack.

"C-come on!" one stammered. "We can take it. There's more of us."

"No!" another cried. "It's driven by the demon. It'll kill us all!"

"We have to kill it first! It killed Claus."

The men approached warily, then abruptly surged forward. Jaeger twisted, striking out with claw and tooth. More than once something sharp penetrated his skin. Pain drove him, and he attacked with a ferocity he had never before experienced. Man after man fell to his anger, to his strength. Blood stained his face, his claws, his fur, coursed through his body, tainted his mind with animal lust. Even when the men drew back, conceding their defeat, Jaeger stalked them. His thoughts tumbled wildly. He wanted them dead, all of them. All who had the audacity to attack him, to injure Rhiannon--

Rhiannon!

Jaeger let out another yowl, then spun and bolted into the darkness. His acute sense of smell led him on the trail of the horse and Rhiannon. He ran through the darkness, legs pumping, heart pounding, until at last he found her.

She had drawn the horse to a stop beside a rocky slope. She sat quietly on the dark rocks but leapt up as he staggered to her and collapsed almost at her feet. He barely had the strength to shapeshift. When he did, he could not suppress a cry of agony. He bled from numerous wounds inflicted by daggers and thrown rocks. There was at least one sword slash down his thigh. It stung like fire.

Rhiannon dropped down on the ground beside him. "Oh, Jaeger," she whispered.

"I'm all right," he managed, looking up at her. "Are you? Your face--"

"My face is fine. It's nothing compared to you!"

"I'm fine," he said again, though pain coursed through him.

She glanced at the sky. "Come on, we have to get you inside before the sun rises."

"Inside?"

"The caves. Look."

Jaeger turned to where she pointed. Several dark openings loomed in the rocks on the slope. He drew a deep breath and got slowly, painfully, to his feet. With Rhiannon's help, he staggered into the chilly darkness. She lowered him gently onto the ground, then turned back toward the opening. He grabbed at her skirt, stopping her.

"Where are you going?"

"I need to find something to burn. It's too cold in here. There's a bit of brush on the hillside."

"Let me fetch it then," he said.

She smiled at him and left. He watched her go with a mixture of love and trepidation, then lay back with a groan. Though his wounds had all ceased bleeding, he was still in pain. He knew, given time to rest, he would recover quickly enough, but he didn't know if he had that time. If Celd was looking for a Bleeder, he was sure to scent the carnage in the village. As sensitive as Jaeger's Vector senses were, Celd's were more so. Naturally, he would investigate.

Jaeger grimaced, remembering how he had torn into the men's flesh. One of them was dead. How many others had succumbed to his fury? The question sent waves of guilt racing through him, mixing with his fear. How could they hunt down someone who had just saved a child's life? It didn't make sense to him. Rhiannon should have been revered, honored, for what she had done. He couldn't leave her now. He had to make sure she was safe, cared for, protected.

He looked up as she re-entered the cave, arms laden with kindling. "Rhiannon, you mentioned you had a clan. Would you like to find them again?"

She shrugged, laying some of the wood into a pile. "If I do, I do. But I am not actively seeking them. Why?"

Jaeger was quiet while she put a spark to the kindling. He watched the flames eat away at the leaves and moss she had stuffed beneath the wood, thinking how alike he and the fire were. Both needed something to feed on to survive, and both destroyed that which provided them life.

Rhiannon looked at him over the small fire. "You want to leave me, don't you?"

The question startled Jaeger, though he knew it shouldn't have. He ought to be getting used to her reading his thoughts, sensing his innermost turmoil. Still, it was a bit disconcerting.

"It's not that I *want* to leave you. But if you stay with me, you'll be in constant danger."

"From?"

He sighed. "From people who despise my kind, from Celd, from me."

She gave him a small smile and moved to sit beside him. Her warm body was welcome and inviting. Jaeger took her into his arms, his heart aching.

"I just don't want you to get hurt," he whispered.

"I won't."

"You already have been." He gently touched the small wound on her face.

"But that wasn't because of you, Jaeger. That was because of me. And you have suffered greatly because of me. If anyone is in danger, it is you."

Jaeger studied her for a moment, then kissed her gently. "If this is danger," he murmured, "then I revel in it."

She giggled and nestled closer to him with a contented sigh. "This is where I want to be, Jaeger. For all time."

"Time," Jaeger repeated. "Time I have too much of. But what about you? I will live on long after you."

"Maybe," she said.

He looked down at her in question. "Do you know something I don't?"

"Maybe," she said again and closed her eyes.

Chapter Ten

They left the next night, both riding the one horse. For the next two weeks, Rhiannon guided them north into the mountains, moving by night, sleeping in caves by day. She seemed familiar with the locale. Her clan called it the Grotto Mountains. She told Jaeger hundreds of caves existed in the hills, some large, some small. She assured him they would easily find shelter whenever they needed it.

Jaeger continuously looked for signs of Rhiannon's people. Though he had not mentioned the clan to her again, he suspected she knew his thoughts.

He had not fed on human blood since attacking the men in the village, and his strength was slowly waning. He didn't think Rhiannon was strong enough to be bled, despite the fact that she had invited him numerous times. In fact, he was worried about her fatigue and pallor. She had become very quiet and spent much of the daylight hours sleeping.

There had been no sign of Celd, for which Jaeger was extremely thankful. Perhaps he had gotten Rhiannon far enough away that the Chosen Vector could no longer sense her, or perhaps Celd had found another to host his child. Whatever the reason, Jaeger had finally relaxed his guard, moving his thoughts from escape to seeking shelter for Rhiannon.

"Jaeger," she said softly. "I need to stop."

He frowned, glancing down at her. She was slumped against him, her face made paler by the moonlight. Dark circles ringed her eyes, which were half-lidded. Jaeger scanned the hillside for one of the caves, and pointed.

"There. That looks like a good place to spend the day." He urged the horse forward.

They reached the site in just moments, but Rhiannon had already sagged into sleep. With one arm, Jaeger secured her small form and dismounted the horse, dragging her with him. She woke with a little gasp, whether of pain or fright, he didn't know. Both concerned him. He touched her forehead.

"You have a fever," he said, his alarm growing.

She looked up at him. "Please, Jaeger, don't reject me further. Please."

"Reject you?" He stared at her in astonishment. "I would never reject you, Rhiannon. You're ill. Come inside, lie down."

He snagged the pack, secured the horse, and led her into what turned out to be quite a large cave.

"Yes, Jaeger, I am ill, but you can help. I need to be bled. Please."

"But you're sick! I can't take your blood when you're sick. It would only make you worse."

"Damn you, Jaeger!" she cried, with all the venom she could manage. "You are making me worse! It's the iron. I have to get rid of it. Please, please, help me." Tears sparkled in her blue eyes, and she clung to him in desperation.

Jaeger drew a deep breath but smelled no iron. He frowned, puzzled. A different scent filled the air, this one sweet and light, yet enticing. He had smelled this before, but he could not say where. It evoked strong memories of his mother, but he could not explain why. With a sigh, he laid the blanket on the cold stone and lowered Rhiannon to it. She pulled him down with her.

He ran one hand through her hair, then brought his lips to meet hers. He was startled by her weak response, almost as if she didn't possess the energy for even a kiss. He drew back to look into her eyes.

"Are you sure?" he asked quietly.

She nodded, and her eyes slid closed. Jaeger hesitated only a moment longer. He brought his mouth to her neck. Her blood tasted different, sweeter, more intoxicating than ever before. He drew on it, savoring the rush it sent through his body, the strength that at once coursed through him.

Rhiannon shuddered, a small sigh of relief escaping her pale lips. Slowly, her arms surrounded him, drew him closer, tighter against her, holding him until he finished.

"Rhiannon?" he said softly.

Her reply was only a sleepy smile. She did not even open her eyes. Jaeger's heart leapt, and he kissed her on the forehead.

"Are you all right? Please, answer me. Say something."

Her eyes fluttered open, the smile never leaving her face. "I love you," she whispered, and fell back into quiet sleep.

Jaeger lay staring at her for a long time, then, carefully, so as to not wake her, he sat up, wrapped the blanket over her.

They had adopted the habit of picking up kindling along the trail, and he fetched their store now. It didn't take long for the dried wood to catch a spark, and soon Jaeger had a respectable fire going. He poured water from the waterskin into a small kettle and set it near the flames to boil, then looked over at Rhiannon.

A smile curved his lips. She loved him. She had spoken the words. He had felt their sincerity. She loved him. It sent his spirits soaring, his mind reeling. At the same time, it plummeted him into despair. They loved each other, but what could ever come of it? A life on the run? As long as she was with him, Celd could find her. He sighed. His father's life all over again, only this time Jaeger was the one running with his beloved.

And what if I leave her? She will still need to be bled to keep from getting ill. Will Celd be able to track her down? Is he still looking? Would someone in her clan be able to protect her? Jaeger didn't think so. Vectors were known for their physical strength as well as their ability to temporarily hypnotize humans. It wouldn't take much to steal her away from her clan.

Jaeger rubbed wearily at his face. It seemed there were no easy answers. Nothing he could do but wait. A noise outside the cave drew his attention, and he rose, peering into the darkness beyond. He saw nothing and was about to reseat himself when a familiar figure appeared in the shadows.

"Hello, Jaeger." Celd's voice snaked through the cold darkness.

Jaeger went rigid, his gut tightening. He could not even manage to utter a greeting as the Vector sauntered his way. Celd's gaze flicked to Rhiannon, who still slept.

"Ah, the Bleeder. So, that's where she went." Celd looked back at Jaeger. "I thought you preferred goat's blood."

"I did," Jaeger managed, then corrected himself, "I do."

Celd chuckled and sniffed the air. "Yet, all I smell here is human blood." He moved closer to the fire and Rhiannon.

Jaeger stepped between them. Celd eyed him with a cold smile. "You did quite a job in that last village you were in. Four men dead, torn apart by some wild, crazed cat. A familiar, some say, to a witch."

Jaeger clenched his jaw to keep from answering. He would not give Celd the satisfaction. The Vector went on, his voice flat, his gaze locked on Rhiannon.

"And this must be the witch. From the barkeep's description, she fits perfectly. A Bleeder and a witch. A charming combination, eh, Jaeg?" He looked to Jaeger, his face gone cold. "She's the one I sought. You knew that. So, why do I now find you with her so many miles from Skyther?" He waited but Jaeger refused to answer. Celd drew a long, slow, irritated breath. "Could it be, Jaeger, that you defied my wishes? That you wish to claim this Bleeder for your own?"

Anger drove Jaeger's response. "She belongs to no one, Celd. Not me nor you."

Celd snorted. "There you are wrong, my boy. As one of the Chosen, I say who belongs to me. And I lay claim to her. Now, run along. I have work to do."

Jaeger stiffened in rage, not moving. Celd's eyebrows rose in surprise. Rhiannon chose that moment to rouse. Her eyes opened slowly, then widened when she saw Celd hovering over her. Clutching the blanket to her, she scooted away. Her gaze darted from Celd to Jaeger and back.

"Jaeger?" she whispered.

"Was just leaving," Celd said.

Jaeger doubled his fists in rage as alarm swept over Rhiannon's face. He looked at Celd. "I am not leaving," he stated calmly. "You are."

Celd drew himself up, seeming to tower over Jaeger, though they were the same height. "I don't think you understand, Jaeger," he said, his voice low and cold. "I have made a choice. You have nothing to say about it. Do I have to remind you of the Sovereign's punishment for disobedience?"

Jaeger swallowed his fear. "I am aware of the Sovereign's punishment.

I'll risk it."

Celd stared at him in open astonishment, then suddenly laughed. He waved one hand through the air, and Jaeger immediately doubled over as excruciating pain tore through him. Rhiannon cried aloud and came to her feet.

"Leave him alone!" she screamed as Jaeger toppled to the ground.

"That's a simple taste of what you'll endure," Celd told Jaeger. "It'll last for days, weeks even. Bit by bit, you'll die, eaten away from the inside. Is she really worth that, Jaeger?"

Jaeger wanted to answer, to say yes, but the pain consumed him, leaving him unable to do more than moan. Rhiannon gripped his arm, addressing Celd.

"Leave him alone," she said again. "Whatever it is you seek of me, then take it. But leave him alone."

"No!" Jaeger managed, but before he could say more, Celd's magic spell claimed him, transporting him away from the cave as easily as a dry leaf in a windstorm.

He landed with a jarring thud on the rocks, barely able to breathe, unable to even stand, still dazed from Celd's web of magic. His gaze flew to the cave. It was only several hundred feet away, but it might as well have been several hundred leagues. Jaeger clawed at the ground, pulling himself forward, inch by inch, even as the night began to recede from the land. The sun touched the horizon, stretching long yellow fingers across the land, reaching for him. Tears stung his eyes. Tears of pain, despair, and rage.

Celd would take Rhiannon, make her his, plant the embryo inside her. She would be lost to Jaeger forever, both in body and spirit. His heart spasmed with his grief, his soul with his loss. He couldn't let this happen. He had to get to her, had to stop Celd.

The sun's first rays reached him, seared his exposed skin, left him gasping for breath. Still he pulled himself forward, ignoring the blisters erupting on his hands and face. A tiny dark hole opened in the ground before him, beckoning with its dark safety. Jaeger lifted his gaze once more to the cave, so far out of reach. Then, with a resigned sob, he used the last of his energy to transform into a snake and slithered into the hole to wait.

Once in the hole, away from the sunlight, and with a smaller body, Jaeger felt renewed energy. He lay still for a moment to gather his strength, then began to follow the narrow tunnel he found. The farther he went, the darker and cooler it was, the better he felt. He moved quickly, his direction straight and true, hoping this small crevice through which he crawled would open into the cavern housing Rhiannon and Celd. What he would do once he got there, he didn't know.

It was obvious he couldn't fight Celd. The Vector was far too strong. At least, he had been. But what if he lost some of that strength by implanting the embryo? What if coupling with Rhiannon left him momentarily fatigued, as it so often did to Jaeger? Then again, Jaeger reminded himself, Celd wasn't a half-breed. He forced the stinging thought aside. Well, if he couldn't best Celd in a battle, then he would...would kill

Rhiannon. He would rather she died quickly at his hands than die a slow, agonizing death at Celd's. The thought turned his blood to ice.

The tunnel sloped upward, and Jaeger shifted to a tiny mountain shrew, better able to grip the slippery ground beneath him. In moments, he emerged into the cave, but he saw no sign of Rhiannon, Celd or the fire. It took him a moment to orient himself, then he scampered toward the mouth of the cave.

He heard them before he saw them. Celd's moans of ecstasy and Rhiannon's cries of pain left no doubt as to what was happening. Jaeger hurried forward, rage tearing through him, but what he saw upon emerging into the front of the cavern sent his anger to white-hot fury.

Celd was atop Rhiannon, holding her down with his magic while he made use of her body as if it were no more than an inanimate object. Jaeger could see the rage and determination on Rhiannon's face as she tried to break free of the Vector's magic by using her own. Jaeger knew what cost she would pay for her effort, and an idea suddenly formed in his mind.

Quickly, he shifted once again; this time to a small brown spider he prayed would be unnoticed. It took him only a moment to cover the distance between himself and Rhiannon. As he hoped, Celd was far too involved in his own pleasures to see him. Rhiannon, however, shifted her gaze, obviously drawn to Jaeger's presence by the strange bond she shared with him.

He crawled forward, seeking shelter in her long tresses that were splayed out on the rock. It took him only a second to reach her skin. Without hesitation, he bit, taking in her iron-rich blood. At once, his energy soared, sending pulses of power racing through him. He backed away, giving himself enough distance to do what he knew he must.

The tiny spider body grew, elongated, and sprouted clawed forearms, strong hind legs, and powerful wings. His head reared upward, his mouth full of razor-sharp teeth, his throat filled with flame and venom. Celd looked up, a gasp escaping him as he scrambled to his feet. For a second, sheer panic crossed his face. It was the second Jaeger needed.

He swept outward with one heavy, clawed arm, raking spiky nails across the Vector's bare chest. Celd stared down as blood spurted from four long gashes. Jaeger didn't wait for him to recover from his shock. He opened his mouth and sent out a stream of fire that swept Celd up in its embrace. The Vector staggered backward, throwing up one arm to shield his face. Jaeger sensed Celd's magic snapping into place, protecting him from, if not exquisite pain, at least death.

With one swift motion, Jaeger snatched Rhiannon from the ground, along with her blanket and the pack, and tucked her safely into one bent arm, then spun and roared from the cave.

The sunlight hit him full in the face, sending agony ripping through his body. Still, he took to the air, his great wings beating the earth into a swirling mass of dirt and debris. Rhiannon's cry echoed against the rocks as Jaeger turned to the mountaintops and the shadows they created with their peaks.

It took him only moments to descend into the gloom, away from the sun, but those moments took their toll. His dragon hide sizzled with blisters, his wings faltered in pain. Still, he flew on, moving as far away from Celd as he could. Finally, he knew he had to stop. He searched out a place he could land that would afford him the darkness he so desperately needed. Finding it at last, he sat down, gently lowering Rhiannon to the ground, then collapsed before her, returning to his Vector form.

Rhiannon grabbed him under the arms and struggled to drag him into the first dark crevice she could find. He lay, shivering, and moaning, both freezing cold and sweating from his numerous burns. Rhiannon touched him gently, tears streaming down her face. He reached up and took her hand in his.

"I'm sorry," he managed, before blackness claimed him.

He woke to the sounds of a crackling fire and the smell of mint. Rhiannon hovered over him, her gentle hands placing cooling gel on his burns. His head swam with dizziness, his gut with nausea, and he managed only a small smile before allowing darkness to claim him once more.

The pattern continued for several days. He would wake for brief moments, always to find Rhiannon there, tending to his injuries. Though he tried desperately to stay awake on those occasions, he found he could not, and would slip back into healing slumber.

Finally, on the fourth day, he was able to do more than merely smile at her. He reached out for her hand, surprised to find it cold and damp. His alarm only grew when he was able to clearly see her face. She was pale, fatigued; yet she gave him a welcoming smile. It was only then that he became aware of the familiar scent.

"You've been using your magic," he murmured. "On me?"

"Some," she replied. "More to shield this place, us."

"From Celd?"

She nodded, a small tremor running through her. He pulled her toward him, and she obliged, lying down and pressing up against his chest. His guilt rose up like bile in the back of his throat.

"Rhiannon," he began softly, "I--"

She shushed him. "It's not your fault," she interrupted.

"Yes, it is. I knew he was looking for you, that he wanted you. I thought I could keep you safe from him. I failed you."

She tipped her head back to look into his eyes. "You failed me? You risked your life for me. How is that failing me?"

"He never should have gotten close. He never should have been able to--" He broke off, his despair gripping him in a cold hand.

"He does not have what he thinks he has."

"He planted the embryo, Rhiannon. Through that, he can command you. I don't know how to stop it, how to stop him."

She shuddered. "I don't want to think about it right now. I want you to help me. I want to help you. It's been too many days, Jaeger. I'm not feeling very well."

He knew what she asked, knew what they both needed, yet was reluctant to act upon it. He wasn't sure how carrying the embryo would affect her, her blood, or him. Again, she seemed to know his thoughts. Tears filled her blue eyes, glittered there like sapphire jewels.

"You no longer want me," she murmured. "I can understand that, Jaeger."

"No," he said at once. "I do want you, Rhiannon. More than anything in the world. But I'm afraid. I'm afraid of doing anything that will show Celd where we are. If I bleed you, Celd may be able to sense it through his bond with the embryo. I don't know much about this, I'm afraid. When I left the Lair years ago, I didn't think to continue studies of my own kind. I'm afraid I am woefully ignorant of a lot of things."

"Then I am trapped." Rhiannon pushed away from him to sit up. "I must be bled, Jaeger, or I will die. If you bleeding me will call Celd here, then I will not risk that. I will go to Celd instead."

Jaeger gasped, gripping her arm. "No!"

"What choice do I have? I cannot keep the shields in place without using more magic. If I use more magic, I increase the iron in my blood. And if I do that, I--" She broke off with a sigh and buried her face in her hands. "I will die."

Jaeger pulled himself to a sitting position beside her. What she said was true, all of it. His gaze danced toward the mouth of the cave. He could see daylight far beyond. Celd couldn't travel in the daylight. It gave Jaeger an idea. He touched Rhiannon's cheek, and she raised her tear-stained face to him.

He tenderly brushed her tears aside, then leaned forward and kissed her lips. They were cool and dry. Her illness was too apparent, and too much for Jaeger to ignore. Without another word, he drew her into his arms to feed upon her blood. She melted into his embrace willingly, eagerly, holding to him even when he was finished.

"I love you, Jaeger," she whispered.

"I love you as well," he told her, stroking her hair. "And if we're to keep that love together, we need to leave this place, now, before Celd is able to travel."

"Now?" She drew back to stare at him in confusion. "But it's daylight outside. You can't go back out there. Not into the sunshine."

"Then I'll keep to the shadows," he told her. "But I'll not let Celd have you." He glanced about for their provisions. "Come, let's get things packed up here."

"Jaeger, I'm not going to let you sacrifice yourself for me," Rhiannon stated firmly. "Not again."

"And I am not going to let you sacrifice yourself to Celd. Now, come on, help me pack up." He rose, heartily strengthened by her sweet-tasting blood. Whereas before it had seemed to fill only a need, now it seemed to do much more. It brought him renewed energy, cleared his thoughts, and gave him a sense of wellness that he had never experienced before. He absently wondered if it was because of the embryo nestled in her womb.

He still didn't know how he was going to keep Celd away from the child, or what he would do with the Vector's baby once it was born. But he had some time to think about it. Not the full nine months he might have with a human child, but, still, he had five months to plan.

He extended his hand to Rhiannon, helping her to her feet. She wore a look of grim resignation.

"Jaeger, how? How can you go out there?"

"It'll be all right. You'll see. Celd told me that as I adjusted to this...this new..." He paused, unsure what to call it, then went on. "Anyway, he told me that I would eventually be able to go back out into the daylight."

"But, then, why can't he?"

"I'm hoping his promotion to one of the Chosen will affect him, just as my...growth is affecting me.

She smiled at his term. "Growth?"

He flushed. "My 'entry into manhood', as you called it."

Rhiannon's eyebrows knotted together, and she took hold of his arm. "You had never lain with a woman before me?"

Jaeger's flush deepened, and he swallowed the lump suddenly forming in his throat. "No." His voice came out in a choked whisper, and he looked away. He was startled by her soft kiss upon his cheek. He dared to look into the blue depths of her eyes, astounded by the love he saw there. Holding the pack with one hand, he pulled her close with the other.

He wanted to make love to her, to show her how much he wanted her, needed her, loved her. His desires were made obvious by his body's youthful reaction to her closeness.

She giggled, though she didn't try to pull away from his embrace. "And shall we use up all of the daylight here?"

He sighed, brought back to cold reality. "No. We can't. We need to keep moving. We need to find someplace safe." Although where that would be, he didn't know. He took her by the hand and led her from the cave.

Chapter Twelve

Jaeger stared morosely into the small fire. He was running out of time. Already he could see a small rounding of Rhiannon's belly. The child was growing. But--so fast? Had Jaeger missed something in Celd's explanation? Had the embryo of the Chosen been magically altered to attain birth even before the usual five short months?

He lifted his gaze toward Rhiannon. Rolled into the only blanket, she rested fitfully, lying on the cold stone floor of a dark cave that had become a backdrop to hers and Jaeger's existence. By the Sovereign, how he wanted a decent inn, a soft bed, and a scented bath in which to luxuriate. And decent food. He was sick of the game animals he brought down in his nightly hunting forays. And Rhiannon needed proper food--fruits, vegetables, milk. She was getting weaker by the day.

They had been walking the cold mountains for almost two weeks, seeing no sign of human life. Fortunately, there didn't seem to be any sign of Celd, either. Still, Jaeger suspected the Vector didn't need to exhaust himself with a search for Rhiannon. All he had to do was wait. His connection to the embryo would draw her to him, not the other way around. He could relax in the comfort and warmth of whatever inn he chose. Eventually, Rhiannon would go to him.

The thought burned in Jaeger's gut, tore his heart to shreds. How could he stand to lose her? How could he turn her over to the likes of Celd? For that matter, to any man? But--how could he stop it? He had thought of going to the Sovereign, of begging for her, but he knew that would only get him the slow death he sought to avoid. No one questioned one of the Chosen.

He rose, walked to the mouth of the cave, and peered out at the lightening lands. They spread before him in their wild beauty--vast fields of wildflowers tumbling down craggy mountain slopes, dotted here and there with stubborn patches of snow. How flowers could bloom in such inhospitable conditions was beyond him.

A quick movement in the grass caught his attention, and he trained his keen eyesight on it. A rabbit! Something he and Rhiannon had not feasted on for weeks, having been relegated to those rodents plentiful in this environment.

He shot a quick glance at Rhiannon, then a quicker one at the skies. If he was very accurate, he might be able to catch the rabbit before the sun rose. Without another thought, he shapechanged into a fox and loped down the hillside, keeping upwind of his prey.

The rabbit, however, was attentive. It stood on powerful hind legs, scanned the immediate area, then, without waiting to see what stalked it, ran. Jaeger went after in hot pursuit. The rabbit led him on a wild chase, careening through brush and flower, over jutting rocks and tangles of berry vines, at last disappearing into a thicket.

Jaeger skittered to a stop, tongue lolling, legs quivering. He peered into the thicket, then drew back. The rabbit was a doe, with young. Jaeger could see the fuzzy heads as she herded them back, away from the fox threatening their existence. Jaeger huffed out a tired breath, turned, and walked away. He would not separate a mother from her young, no matter his hunger.

The first, feeble rays of morning sunshine caught him off-guard and still quite a distance from the cave. He glanced up, then broke into a run, driving his exhausted body forward. A sudden shriek from overhead sent him belly-flat to the ground. His gaze shot to an enormous hawk sailing quietly over the wakening lands. Too tired to shapeshift, Jaeger pressed himself into the flowers and waited.

This was no ordinary hawk, of that he was sure, though he was just as sure it wasn't Celd. A few more moments would tell. If the hawk beat a hasty retreat as the sun reached over the land, Jaeger would get his answer.

There was something familiar about the feel of the hawk, something Jaeger couldn't quite decipher. His gaze drifted to the mouth of the cave, than back to the horizon. If he didn't move soon, he would be caught in the morning sun. Though he was better acclimated to daylight, he knew he couldn't withstand its full onslaught. Yet, if this hawk was indeed one of Celd's minions he wasn't going to lead it directly to Rhiannon, either. So, he waited.

Finally, the hawk gave another screech and winged away, disappearing into the shadows of the mountains. Jaeger hesitated, then began to creep toward the cave and safety. He barely made it. The sun rose just as he slipped into the welcoming darkness and returned to his Vector form. He collapsed against the stonewall and sagged to the ground. Footfalls brought him upright again with a gasp.

A tall, thin form slipped from the darkness to greet him. "Jaeger! Where the hell have you been? I've been looking all over for you!"

"Darius?" Jaeger pushed away from the wall, overwhelmed with both relief and fear. He stared at the man standing before him. Darius was at least twice his age, had been a mentor and a friend for decades. He was also an Elder Chosen, someone who held rank over Jaeger. And right now, Jaeger saw disapproval and anger in the dark eyes.

"Yes, Darius!" the Vector snapped, approaching him. "What do you mean by attacking one of the Chosen?"

Jaeger cringed under the biting tone, ran one hand through his hair and shook his head.

"I don't know, Elder," he admitted, his voice soft.

"You don't know?" Darius bellowed, his voice echoing in the caves.

Rhiannon came awake with a startled cry. Upon seeing Darius standing before Jaeger, she grabbed up her blanket and backed away. Jaeger's heart broke at the terror he saw reflected in her blue eyes. Ignoring Darius, he went to comfort her.

"Who is he?" she whispered, clinging to his arm.

"Darius, an Elder, and an old friend," Jaeger replied quietly.

"A friend? Of yours or Celd's?"

Jaeger hesitated, not quite sure how to answer that. He suspected that Darius had heard the question, and he turned his gaze back to see the other Vector's reaction. Darius was studying Rhiannon with open interest.

"So, this is the wench causing all the problems?" he asked.

"She is no wench," Jaeger said at once.

"No." Darius moved closer, his gaze narrowing in thought. "She *is* a Bleeder and a witch, however. A pleasing combination. No wonder Celd chose her." He moved closer still. "And quite lovely as well." His gaze moved to Jaeger. "I can see your attraction, Jaeger. She does seem to have a lot to give."

Desperation tore through Jaeger. "Darius, please, say nothing. Don't let Celd have her. Please. I--I love her. I can't bear the thought of Celd--" He broke off, a lump forming in his throat.

Darius looked at Rhiannon again. "And you, do you also love Jaeger?"

Rhiannon seemed surprised he should even address her. She nodded. "Very much."

"And how long did you track him before you claimed him?" Darius asked.

Jaeger frowned in confusion, but a little gasp escaped Rhiannon. Her eyes grew wide, and her gaze darted from Darius to Jaeger.

He shook his head. "What do you mean, tracked me?"

"I...I..." For the first time, Rhiannon seemed to be at a loss for words.

Jaeger looked to Darius. "What do you mean?"

Darius settled his lithe form on the floor by the fire and fixed his dark gaze on Rhiannon. "Why don't you tell him why you might want him?"

Jaeger sat as well, paying homage to this Vector before him, then looked at Rhiannon. "Yes, please, tell me."

She sighed. "I...I had sensed a Vector was in the area. I..." She drew a deep breath, then rushed on. "I followed you through a city and two villages, Jaeger, before I caught up with you. At least, I think it was you. In retrospect, it could have been Celd."

"But why? Why were you following me?"

Again, she hesitated. "Because of what I am, because of what you are. I knew we could benefit each other."

"Benefit?" Jaeger moved away from her, not sure how to analyze the conflicting emotions leaping inside. "Like a partnership? A business?"

"No!" Rhiannon cried. "No, it's not like that at all!"

"Then what is it?" he asked. "You sought me out to help you with your affliction. That was all?"

Rhiannon stiffened. "My affliction. Is that what you call this curse? My 'affliction'?"

His own anger was on the rise. "It is no different than my curse, Rhiannon!"

"Exactly! That's why I thought we could help each other."

Jaeger surged to his feet, quite forgetting about Darius. "Help each other? Become partners? Associates in a business deal? Thank you, Rhiannon! Thank you for taking what I perceived as love and making it nothing more than a...than a..." He threw up his hands, not sure what words would adequately express what he was feeling.

"That's not fair, Jaeger!" she seethed. "It's true that I did not approach this with anything more than a partnership in mind, but it has become much more than that."

Jaeger wasn't listening. His anger and hurt had closed off his understanding. He spun away from her. "If you only wish a partnership, then you shall have one. With Celd. You'll be treated as a queen, Rhiannon. He is, after all, one of the Chosen. His father is High Chancellor. He's practically a prince in the Lair! And you, after all, do carry his child."

Darius let out a gasp of surprise. He jerked his gaze to Jaeger. "What? Celd has already implanted the embryo?"

"Yes," Jaeger snapped, again forgetting just whom he spoke to. "More than a month ago."

"Then why is she here? Why is she not with Celd?"

Rhiannon exploded with fury. She raged to her feet and grabbed up the cloak. "I'll not be with any man unless I choose to be!" she spat.

"Where are you going?" Jaeger demanded.

"None of your business! This 'partnership', as you so coldly label it, has ended!" She stormed out of the cave into the sunshine.

His anger snuffed out, Jaeger rushed forward, only to be stopped by the blinding glare of the sun on bare rock. He shielded his face. "Rhiannon! Come back! You can't go off alone! Please, come back!"

There was no answer, and Jaeger spun in panic toward Darius. "Please, Elder, go after her. Bring her back."

Darius sighed. "I cannot. Even for me that sunlight is too intense. I fear we'll have to wait until evening."

"Rhiannon!" Jaeger called again, then again, and again, until his voice was hoarse and raw. She did not return.

Chapter Thirteen

Darius waited a moment, then rose and approached Jaeger. He hesitated before reaching out and drawing Jaeger into his embrace. The unexpected action, the paternal touch, only served to further Jaeger's heartache, and he very nearly collapsed into Darius' arms. The older Vector led him back to the fire and urged him to sit.

"This love," he said at length, "this love you feel for this woman, what do you think it is?"

Jaeger scrubbed at his eyes, shaking his head. "What do you mean?"

"Well," Darius said slowly, "you have only just come into your Growth. From what Celd told me, you have experienced human blood and the human body for the first time."

Understanding crept over Jaeger. "You mean, do I love her or simply lust after her?"

Darius nodded. "The two can oftentimes become confused in the young."

Jaeger snorted. "I am hardly young, Darius. I should think I would know love when it hits me full in the face."

"It is not your face I am wondering about," Darius said.

Jaeger felt the color rush to his cheeks, and he averted his gaze. "Yes, I have experienced Rhiannon as a woman. More than once. I don't believe that affects my feelings for her, except to strengthen them. I love her, Darius. She claims a part of my heart that will belong to no other."

"And will you love her still when she births Celd's child?"

Jaeger drew a slow breath. "Yes, though I am not sure what we will do with the child once it is born. It will die unless it feeds on blood within hours of its birth, yet I cannot willingly force Rhiannon to supply that blood. Better that it dies."

Darius was quiet a moment before speaking. "If it dies, your life will be forfeit. You know that."

Jaeger felt a shiver of trepidation run through him. "My life is forfeit now," he replied. "I attacked one of the Chosen. I stole away an impregnated hostess. I defied the Lair and the Sovereign. Just as my father did." He eyed Darius with a sigh. "I don't believe your presence here is an accident, or because of your undying friendship for me. Are you here as Darius, friend, or Darius, Elder?"

Darius grimaced, though true hurt flickered through his dark eyes. Jaeger winced and mumbled soft apologies.

"You're right," Darius said at length. "In some things. I was sent to find you, to take you back to the Lair for your punishment. But that issue is a bit clouded by my closeness with you, and with your father. When he was...banished...and your mother killed, I took it upon myself to look after you. Apparently, I have not done such a wonderful job."

Jaeger let out a wry chuckle. "My father. I hadn't talked of him for years. Now he seems to be in every waking thought. I guess what they say is true after all. Like father, like son. He was banished for loving my mother and letting her live after my birth, for protecting her those long seven years while they ran from the Sovereign. In the end, it served neither of them. He was banished, she was killed. And me, I live in their shadows, trying to forget one and trying to always remember what the other told me." He rose to pace. "Now, here I am, attempting to protect another human from the same fate." He looked at Darius. "So, when will we return to the Lair? What will my punishment be? The slow death Celd outlined? Or is there something far worse?"

"The High Chancellor has left it up to me." Darius paused, then continued in answer to Jaeger's questioning glance. "There are some benefits to being as old as I am, and with having implanted as many embryos as I have."

"This can't be easy for you," Jaeger said. "I suspect there is a bit of punishment being dealt to you as well. Perhaps for allowing me to follow my mother's wishes in regards to my feeding preferences all of these years?"

Darius was quiet for a moment as he studied Jaeger's face. "Perhaps. Still, I know the pain you are experiencing, Jaeger. One of my children was also in love with a human. He paid dearly for that love. I don't want to see the same thing happen to you."

Jaeger looked at him in surprise. "I didn't know that."

Darius gave a wry smile. "There are many things about me that you do not know, Jaeger. For one, I am not in agreement with all that our Sovereign says and does. I do not condone the use of hostesses to bear Vector children. I see no point in it, to be honest, other than saving the shape of a Vector mother. And, believe it or not, there are plenty who agree with me." He tossed another small piece of kindling onto the fire. "And I do not agree with the punishment he has outlined for you."

"And that punishment is what?" Jaeger asked, his heart pounding.

Darius sighed, as if unwilling to voice the awful truth. "I will not take you back to the Lair, Jaeger. I don't need to. What must be done, will be done here. But it will be on my terms, not the Sovereign's."

"You risk much, Elder," Jaeger said quietly.

Darius shrugged, no sign of worry on his face.

Jaeger shifted uncomfortably, wishing Darius would just get on with it, and yet wishing he wouldn't. "One thing, Darius. Don't let Celd have Rhiannon. Please. If he must claim the child, then so be it, but please don't let him have her."

Darius studied Jaeger for a long moment. "That will be up to you," he said finally.

Jaeger started to question him, but was suddenly seized with agonizing pain. It tore through his body, ripped into his soul, left his mind numb with confusion and alarm. His eyesight blurred, dimmed, then disappeared completely. Cold gripped him, set his teeth chattering, his body shuddering. He felt himself crumple, felt the cold stone beneath him, felt his cheek strike rock, but could do nothing to stop his fall. He lay paralyzed with both pain and terror. Darius' voice came to him as if down a long tunnel.

"The punishment is complete," he said softly. "In time, you will accept it. In time, you will understand. And perhaps this is for the best, Jaeger. I will not lose you, too."

Jaeger trembled, welcoming the veil of blackness that finally descended over him.

He woke to nightfall and silence. His head pounded with pain, his stomach rumbled with hunger. He stretched, then frowned. He didn't feel right. He turned his head, and a low yowl escaped him. He was no longer a man. Four heavy paws were where hands and feet should have been, attached to a muscular body that bore not skin and clothing, but fur. Sleek, shiny, black fur that picked up the brilliant moonlight from beyond the cave and splintered into dozens of colors.

Jaeger rolled and came dizzily to his feet. He tried to shapeshift back to his Vector form and found he could not. Panic replaced the confusion. He tried again and met with the same failure.

He was trapped in the body of a mountain cat.

Realization came slowly to his fogged mind. Darius had done this. This was his punishment. He was no longer of either the human or Vector world. He was an animal. And, most likely, destined to stay that way forever. His father had suffered the same punishment. *How fitting*, he thought now, *to follow in his father's footsteps so literally*. Perhaps he would be hunted down and shot. Someday his skin might hang above a mantle or warm the floor before a hearth. With an inward shudder, he padded silently to the mouth of the cave.

A cold wind blew, ruffling the tops of the grass and flowers. Jaeger lifted his head and sniffed. His senses as a Vector had always been acute; now, as a mountain cat, they were even more so. His tufted ears swiveled, picking up sounds too quiet for any but another animal to hear. His eyesight cut through the darkness, able to see shape and form, though not color in the dim light outside. His stomach again reminded him that he was hungry.

He left the cave quietly, not looking back. It was over, his life as Jaeger the Vector. There was little sense in dwelling on it. His thoughts went to Rhiannon; and just as quickly he tore them away, pushing them to the far corners of his mind. There was even less sense in thinking about her. She was lost to him forever. Not only was she carrying a Vector child that would insure her slavery to Celd, but she could certainly never love the animal that Jaeger had become. He increased his gait, loping down the mountainside, on the watch for anything he could catch to take the dull ache from his belly.

He found a ground squirrel. The chase was brief, easy, over in a heartbeat. Jaeger tore into the dead animal, gulping down mouthfuls of raw meat, licking the red blood from his paws and claws. He felt revitalized, energetic, but not satiated. He continued to prowl for something more substantial. As he walked, he assimilated his predicament, puzzled at his own calm acceptance of it.

He knew what to expect, though how he knew was beyond him. Perhaps Darius had gifted him with an explanation, given while he lay unconscious on the floor of the cave. Like his father, he was trapped inside this animal body, unable to speak yet retaining the intellect and emotions of a man. It was banishment like no other. Doomed to a life of solitude, he would wander forever. A shudder ran through him at the thought, and he quickened his pace. How could Darius have chosen this particular punishment for him? He had thought of the Vector as a friend, almost a father. On the other hand, he guessed no one really had a friend once they had defied the Sovereign. Still...he tried to snort, let out a low growl instead, and startled away a jackrabbit exploring outside its burrow.

Jaeger darted forward, batted at the burrow opening, then began to dig, sudden anger driving his actions. He knew he wouldn't catch the rabbit, but he didn't care. He only wanted to release the rage that festered inside him. Dirt and rocks flew from his strong paws, filled the air with dust and bits of grass. The debris settled over his black coat, gritted in his eyes, soured his tongue. It was only when he was thoroughly exhausted, drained of his anger that he stopped.

He sat back on his haunches, head hanging. If he had still been a man, he would have wept. But he wasn't. And would never be again.

He struggled to his feet and once more began to walk. He kept to the mountains, wondering if he would be able to survive in the daylight, wondering if Darius had left him with that Vector curse. If so, he would need a place of refuge, a place to hide until night came again. Though why he bothered keeping alive, he didn't know. Or did he?

The thought hit him hard, stopping him in his tracks. Rhiannon. She was why he had to stay alive. He had to find her, protect her. If Celd showed up--Jaeger's cat eyes narrowed to mere slits--he would kill the Vector. Somehow.

He increased his gait to a lope. He would find her, return her to the cave where she had left the supply pack, watch over her until the child was born. And then? He shook the dirt from his fur. He didn't know what he would do, didn't know what course of action he would take. But he was sure of one thing--he would not let Celd have Rhiannon.

He began to run, his long muscles rippling beneath his fur, propelling him over the ground effortlessly. He tested the air constantly, seeking out the scent that would lead him to her. He slowed only when his acute senses were overwhelmed with it, the sweet, intoxicating scent that was Rhiannon. He moved ahead slowly, cautiously, his gaze flicking over the dark terrain. Finally, he saw her.

She sat, back against a boulder, cloak drawn tight, chin resting on her knees. The moonlight kissed her tousled hair, and Jaeger remembered running his fingers through it. He remembered how soft it was, how it curled about his bare chest and shoulders as they had made love. The thoughts cut into his heart, and he shuddered, willing them away.

Silently, he approached her, then stopped when she lifted her head and gasped. Her face was wet, her tears glittering like silver jewels in the moonlight. He took another step toward her, but stopped when he saw her stiffen in alarm. For a long moment, she watched him, her brow furrowing in puzzlement.

Jaeger wasn't sure what to do. It was obvious she didn't know him. Whatever it was that had allowed her to see him before no matter what shape he took, apparently was now gone. Still, she didn't seem unduly frightened of him. More like wary. He lay down in the dust, placing his head between his front paws, and looked up at her.

"Well," she whispered. "What now?"

Jaeger briefly closed his eyes at the sound of her voice. He wanted to be next to her, to dry her tears, to ease her fears, to somehow make her know who he was. He opened his eyes, hoping beyond hope she could see past the animal.

Her frown deepened. "What do you want with me? If you wish to make a meal of me, then do so. Get it over with. I've nothing left to live for, anyway."

Her words cut into his heart. He lifted his head, a soft mew escaping him. Even though he knew she didn't understand, she still spoke as if she did.

"Oh? The child?" She laid one hand on her belly. "Yes, there is the child to think about, isn't there? But it's not mine. It belongs to someone else, and I won't be able to keep it. And...and..." Her tears resurfaced.

Jaeger responded instinctively, moving up next to her. She cried out in terror, pressing herself against the rock. Jaeger leaned forward and gently licked the tears from her cheeks. She let out a soft squeal, but he persisted.

"So," she said, her voice trembling. "Are you simply tasting me for later?"

It would have made him laugh had he been a man. Now, the best he could do was rub his head against her chin, hoping she would understand. When he drew back, she regarded him curiously. Slowly, she reached up and placed one hand on each side of his face, then peered into his dark eyes. He remained still, praying she would at last see who he truly was.

"Jaeger?" she breathed, then shook her head. "No. No, you would change back." She released him with a heavy sigh.

Jaeger's gut flipped. Yes! He wanted to scream. Yes, it's me! Please, Rhiannon, see that. Please. He shook his head from side to side and placed one large paw on her arm. She managed a small smile.

"You certainly are a friendly one," she said, reaching out to stroke him between the ears. "I could use a friend about now." She paused, glancing around. "I don't suppose you know where I could find some food, or a place to sleep?"

Jaeger leapt away from her, then back, then again away.

Rhiannon watched his wild antics, then rose. "Should I go with you, then?" She shrugged. "What do I have to lose? Except maybe my life."

Jaeger came to her side and gently gripped the edge of her cloak in his mouth. He tugged at it, forcing her to take several steps alongside him. She nodded and followed along obediently.

They walked the rest of the evening, Jaeger leading the way, prodding her when she slowed or stopped. Her fear of him, of what he might do, kept her moving. As morning broke, they finally came within sight of the cave. Rhiannon seemed too tired to notice she was in a familiar place as she sagged to a boulder to rest. Jaeger glanced at the sky, then tugged again at her cloak.

"Please," she begged. "I need to stop. I'm tired."

Jaeger pulled harder, but she ignored him. Finally, he spun and bolted the remaining distance to the cave. Once inside, he grabbed up the pack with his teeth, then raced back to where Rhiannon waited. She let out a loud gasp when he dropped the pack at her feet. Her gaze shot to his face.

"Jaeger!" she cried, falling to her knees before him. "By the gods, it is you! Why don't you change? Why are you staying in this form?" She wrapped her arms around his neck and hugged him.

Jaeger closed his eyes in relief and nestled against her.

Chapter Fourteen

Rhiannon stared at him over the flickering flames of their campfire. She had finally made it into the cave and rekindled the fire. Jaeger hadn't risked going outside yet, wasn't even sure if he could. He was content just to know where Rhiannon was, that she was safe and that she was aware of who he was. He wished he could explain to her what had happened. She had asked time and again, obviously expecting he would soon change back to his Vector form and answer her pleas.

Now, she had lapsed into silence, merely watching him. It was almost more than he could stand. He sprang up and padded over to press against her. She absently reached up to stroke his furred head.

"You can't, can you?" she finally asked. "That other Vector did this, didn't he? Because of me?"

Jaeger stared at her, astounded at her perception. She wiped furiously at tears that trickled down her cheeks.

"This is all my fault. If I had not sought you out in the first place, none of this would have happened." She gave a grim laugh. "And you believed it was I who was in danger being with you. It was surely the other way round."

Jaeger sighed and rubbed his furred head gently against her shoulder.

She glanced sideways at him, swallowing hard. "We need to come up with some sort of language, Jaeger. I need some way to talk to you, to understand you." She paused, studying him. "You can nod and shake your head, right? So, at least we have yes and no. And I think I understand when you want me to move." She gave him a wry smile, then her shoulders sagged. "But I just want to hear your voice again. I want to feel your touch again. And--and I want to apologize. I should have expected you to be upset with me. I should have told you that I was following you from the start. I'm sorry."

Jaeger placed one paw on her knee and shook his head. She frowned.

"No? I shouldn't have told you?"

He tried again, this time nodding. That only served to increase her confusion and brought fresh tears.

"I'm not going to be able to take this, Jaeger," she sobbed. "I need you as a man. I need you to hold me, to be with me. I need to know you forgive me for causing this. Even if you don't want to bleed me anymore, I still need your touch."

Jaeger started. He had quite forgotten about the bleeding. She would still need to be bled, to lose the extra iron that her pregnant body was creating. How could he help her now? He leaned against her, rubbing his cheek against hers in a comforting gesture, though he was far from comforted himself.

She clung to him, sobbing, then abruptly reeled dizzily. He lay down, his action pulling her with him. She lay still, trying to get her tears under control.

"I don't feel well, Jaeger," she mumbled.

Help, he thought. You need human help. Something I can't give you. Decent food, someplace warm to rest. The clan! If only he could get her to her clan. He slipped from her grasp and went to the entrance of the cave. Rhiannon watched him with open alarm.

"What are you doing? Where are you going? You can't leave me here, Jaeger!"

He glanced back at her, then walked slowly out into the sunshine. Relief coursed through him. It didn't burn, didn't so much as make his eyes water. He could be outside in the daylight! He sent a heartfelt mental thank you to Darius, then whirled and dashed back inside, his euphoria guiding him. Rhiannon sat up slowly, watching him as he grabbed up the pack. He dropped it near her, then darted back toward the cave opening.

"We're leaving?" she asked, wiping her face dry on her sleeve. "And going where?"

Jaeger could see no way to answer that. But it was enough that she understood his suggestion to leave. He went back to the pack. Using his teeth and claws, he managed to open up a laced pouch on the back. Rhiannon peered into it.

"Money?" She looked up at him. "A village? You want me to go to a village, don't you?"

He bobbed his head up and down, then on impulse, licked her full on the lips. She pushed him away, and gave a shaky laugh.

"They will never let you in, you know. In fact, if they see me waltz into town with a black mountain cat as a companion, they'll have me hanging for witchcraft in moments. Have you thought of that?"

In fact, he had. At least, the part about not being able to go inside an inn with her. He hadn't really thought about the witch part of it. Still, he thought, if he could just get her close enough to a village, she could do the rest. He could wait for her in the outskirts. He nudged her.

"Wait," she said, her smile disappearing. "What will I do about my blood? This child--it seems to be forcing my body to produce more iron than it normally would. I need to be bled, Jaeger. Who will do that for me?"

Jaeger sat back for a moment. Then, slowly, he rose and went to her. He nuzzled against her neck, then licked it several times. Rhiannon sighed and wrapped her arms about him.

"If I close my eyes, Jaeger," she whispered, "I can still sense you. The man inside the beast."

He heard the tremor in her voice, knew that tears had once more filled her eyes. Heartache gripped him. He would have cried as well, if only he could. Instead, he bared his fangs, then quickly, expertly, bit into her neck. She gave a brief cry of pain, something she had never done before, but she did not relax her hold on him.

Her blood was warm, sweet, exotic. He licked it away as fast as it flowed, reveling in the strength it gave him, in the heightened emotions it fueled him with. When it stopped, he let out a soft growl of disapproval and bit again. This time Rhiannon's cry of pain echoed in the cavern, startling him. He backed away, his eyes widening, his body trembling. Rhiannon reached up to her neck and brought back a hand covered with her own blood. She looked at Jaeger in confusion.

Repulsed by his own actions, Jaeger backed further away. What was happening to him? What was this sudden urge to taste flesh?

"Jaeger?" Rhiannon's voice was soft, not angry.

Grief-stricken, Jaeger spun and bounded from the cave. He tore down the mountainside, blinded by his own despair. So, this was what he had to look forward to? Having the emotions and intellect of a man, yet the primitive instincts of an animal? To be able to know how his prey was feeling, even as he tore them to pieces? He raced on, ignoring the fatigue pressing against him, threatening to drop him. He could kill her. He would, if he stayed with her. Yet, how could he leave her?

His gait slowed; and at last he stopped, sides heaving, tongue lolling from his mouth. He needed water. Not to drink, but to end his life. Just as his father had done. Now, Jaeger understood what had driven his father to leap into raging rapids, to allow himself to be dragged under, to suffer a horrible death. There was little that could kill a Vector, but drowning was one thing that was very reliable.

Anger slowly replaced the exhaustion running through him. Jaeger let out a long, low yowl that floated eerily over the flower fields. He needed to hunt, he needed to eat, and he needed blood. It wouldn't be Rhiannon he would feast on. Resolve guiding him, he rose and once more went on the prowl.

He returned to the cave to find Rhiannon gone. She had taken the pack with her and left an arrow made of sticks. The sight of it lightened his mood. She apparently wanted him to follow, despite the fact that he had just tried to tear her throat open. He turned and quietly followed her trail.

It didn't take him long to catch up to her. She was struggling along a slope of loose shale, holding to whatever she could find to brace her footing. Jaeger watched her a moment, then slipped up next to her. Her relief at seeing him was obvious.

"Oh, Jaeger," she breathed, collapsing to the rock to hug him. "I was afraid you wouldn't come back."

He tried to avoid looking at the dried blood on her neck, but couldn't help himself. She noticed and rubbed at the wound.

"I understand. Believe me, I do. I'm not angry with you. Don't be angry with yourself. Please."

And who should I be angry with? he wondered. Tentatively, he touched the wound with his tongue, and licked the blood away. Rhiannon sat very still, not challenging him, though she trembled. She seemed as relieved as he when the cleaning did not spur him to once more take a bite. She managed a shaky smile.

"Thank you. And, just so you'll know, the bleeding did make me feel better." She got to her feet and once more took up the pack. "Do you have any idea in which direction there might be a village?"

Jaeger shook his head and fell into step beside her. More than once she slipped on the shale, but always he was there with his muscular body to stop her fall. By nightfall, they still had not reached a village, but Jaeger's keen sense of smell caught the scent of cooking meat. He peered ahead into the darkness, finally spotting a dark huddle of buildings in the distance. The faint glow of lamplight and the wispy tendrils of smoke brought him vast relief. He looked up at Rhiannon, concerned by her pallor and quite noticeable fatigue.

He gave a low rumble, drawing her attention, then turned his head in the direction of the buildings. Rhiannon followed his gaze.

"A farm," she mumbled. Though relief was in her voice, her steps faltered. "Do you think it will be safe?"

Jaeger bobbed his head, then let out a soft growl. Rhiannon looked down at him with a small smile.

"You'll be there? With me?" She gave a light laugh. "And you think the owner will let me in with you at my side?"

Jaeger saw her point, but was determined to stay close. He would let no harm befall her. Not now, not ever. He nudged her on, thinking only of her comfort for the night.

Rhiannon sighed and walked on. They reached the house not much later, and Jaeger prodded Rhiannon to the door. She cast him a tentative glance as he slunk to the shadows, then she knocked on the wooden door. It was a moment before it was opened. Jaeger peered up at the man from his hiding place.

He was older, almost bald, with sagging jowls, and watery brown eyes. He was dressed in a nightshirt hanging to his ankles, but gaping open at his broad chest. He seemed startled to see a young, pregnant woman standing on his doorstep.

"Sir," Rhiannon began, her voice wavering. "I was wondering if you would be so kind as to let me have a stall in which to spend the night?"

Jaeger started. A stall! No! He wanted her bedded down properly, with a bath beforehand and a good hot meal in her stomach.

The man opened his mouth to answer, but at that moment, Rhiannon swayed dizzily and caught at the doorjamb to keep from toppling. The man grabbed her.

"Here, now, young miss," he said. "You look like you could use a damn sight more than a stall. Come on inside. Easy now." He led her into the house and shut the door.

Jaeger felt just a flicker of concern rush through him. He crept alongside the house until he reached a window that was left un-shuttered. He pulled himself up with his front paws on the sill and peeked inside. The man had led Rhiannon to a chair before the fire and was ladling out a cup of soup from a pot over the hearth. He presented it to her, then busied himself with cutting bread, his mouth moving in conversation the whole time.

Rhiannon glanced about the room, her gaze finally meeting Jaeger's. She gave a small, wary smile of acknowledgment, then returned her attention to the man. Satisfied she would be cared for, Jaeger continued his investigation of the house, inspecting each window. He wanted to be near her, to be able to respond at a moment's notice. It wasn't much later he saw the lamplight move to one of the back windows. He followed, once more rising up on his hind legs to peer inside the room.

The man was motioning Rhiannon to a low bed piled with blankets. He tipped his head, then took his leave, closing the door behind him. Rhiannon went immediately to the window and opened it.

"Will you come inside?" she whispered.

Jaeger shook his head, and licked her cheek gently. It wouldn't be safe, but how he yearned to be next to her, to feel her arms about him, her warm body pressed against his. Once again, he felt the pain of his situation, the shattering heartbreak of his entrapment. Hers appeared to be no less. With tears glimmering in her blue eyes, she leaned forward and kissed him gently on the forehead, then closed the window and went to bed.

Jaeger watched for a few moments, then dropped down in the dirt below the window. He curled into a ball, shivering in the cold night air, tucked his head into his paws, and dreamt of raging rivers and an end to his torment.

Chapter Fifteen

aeger woke to sounds of movement, someone arriving at the farm on horseback. He lifted his head, sniffing the air. Scents of ale, pipe smoke, and sweat set his nerves on edge and raised the fur along his back. He got stiffly to his feet and reared up to peer into Rhiannon's bedroom. It was pitch black, the lamp having been put out long ago, yet Jaeger could see her sleeping beneath tangles of blankets. He dropped back to all four feet and padded silently around the corner of the house. Nothing moved.

Senses still on the alert, Jaeger continued his patrol like a black shadow, completely circling the house. He returned to Rhiannon's window just as he heard her muffled cry of alarm. Immediately, he sprang to look inside. A low growl erupted from his throat.

A man had entered her room. Not the old man. This one was younger, more muscular. He sat on the edge of Rhiannon's bed, holding her against him with one hand, the other tight over her mouth to prevent her from calling out. She struggled against him, trying in vain to wrestle free as he forced her down upon the bed, covering her body with his as he pushed up her nightshirt.

Jaeger dropped to the ground, backed up, then flung himself against the window. It shattered, sending wood and glass flying. He landed on the floor of the bedroom, his fur raised, a roar of fury erupting from his throat.

The man rolled away from Rhiannon, toppling to the floor in his haste. She scrambled off the bed in the other direction, her eyes wide with fear. Jaeger let out another low, throaty growl, his gaze fixed on the man, who now scuttled backward in terror. The door to the bedroom crashed open; and the older man stumbled inside, rubbing sleep from his eyes. His gaze flew to Jaeger, and the color drained from his face. He turned and bolted.

Jaeger lowered his head, taking another step toward the younger man sprawled on the floor. Rage burned in Jaeger's gut. He drew his mouth back to reveal sharp, white teeth and advanced another step. Rhiannon's cry of warning stopped him. His gaze darted upwards. The old man had returned to the doorway and had an arrow trained on him.

"No!" Rhiannon screamed, coming to her feet.

Jaeger sprang just as the arrow hissed from the bow. He felt the impact on his rear flank as the arrow embedded in muscle. Yowling in pain, he struck the old man, knocking him to the floor. Then, seizing the bow in his mouth, he disarmed his attacker with one powerful twist. "Jaeger!" Rhiannon screamed at him. "Go! Run! I can handle this!"

He felt her shoving him from behind. He staggered into the main room, pain flaring through his hip. Rhiannon brushed past him to fling open the front door.

"Go!' she shrieked. "I'll find you!"

He looked up into her eyes, then fled, trailing blood in his wake. He got as far as the barn, where he staggered into a stall and collapsed into the hay. His hip was on fire, his whole body trembling with agony. He hoped his Vector blood would sustain him now, would heal him. He twisted, jerked the arrow from his flesh with his teeth, and began to lick his wound, letting his animal instincts take over.

Once the bleeding had slowed, he rose, wincing in pain. He was not about to run off and leave Rhiannon at the mercy of those two men. While he still trusted the older man, he harbored only hatred for the younger one. Silently, he crept from the barn and slipped through the darkness back toward the house. He heard voices as he drew nearer.

"What were you doing?" the older man bellowed.

"Trying to keep that animal from attacking her!" The younger man's voice was slurred with drink.

"Liar!" Rhiannon screamed.

"Be still, wench!" The older man's voice was sharp, cold, and commanding.

Jaeger stole to the window and peered inside. The younger man was slumped in a chair, his face still ashen, while the older man paced angrily before the hearth. Rhiannon sat at the table, her back stiff, eyes glowing with rage.

"Are you going to believe her?" the younger man snapped. "A witch?"

The older man stopped abruptly and spun to face Rhiannon. "Are you?" he demanded. "Are you a witch?"

"Oh, please, father! It doesn't take much to see that. You saw how she commanded that cat. She called it by name. It did her bidding. Likely she was expecting it to kill us both so she could have the house and land."

"If I had wanted him to kill you," Rhiannon seethed, "he would have."

The old man looked from one to the other, then ran a thick hand through his already-tousled hair. "Well, I'll not have it," he mumbled. "I'll not have a witch staying in this house. You gather your things, missy, and you get."

"You can't let her go!" the younger man cried, surging to his feet. "She's a witch! She should be hanging from the gallows, not traipsing about the countryside terrorizing decent folks."

"Shut up!" the old man roared at his son. He looked again at Rhiannon. "Get your things."

She rose, shot a quick glance at the younger man, and went into the bedroom. Jaeger raced around the side of the house to the broken window. She noticed him at once. Quickly, she slipped from the nightshirt the man had given her and dressed in her own clothes. She grabbed the pack, flinging it out the window over Jaeger's head. Without a word, she slipped over the sill and dropped to the ground. She gave Jaeger a brief hug, then snatched up the pack, and the two of them melted into the darkness.

Jaeger heard the old man hollering for her to hurry up, then his cry of surprise to find her already gone.

"How dare he?" Rhiannon murmured, her steps fast and furious. "How dare he touch me?"

Jaeger limped alongside her, trying to ignore the pain that flared through him with each step. He only wanted to put some distance between them and the two men. Guilt brought him almost as much pain as his injury. He never should have taken her there, never should have trusted another man to protect her, to care for her. But, he was not going to be able to do it. He knew that. He wished with all his heart he could find her clan, return her to their safekeeping; yet he knew he was not going to be able to do that, either. With a heavy sigh, he followed her as she moved at a steady pace back toward the Grotto Mountains and the caves.

Her steps finally faltered at dawn, her anger spent. She stopped, letting the pack fall to the ground. Jaeger limped up beside her and gingerly eased himself to a sitting position. Rhiannon glanced down at him, then collapsed beside him in tears. She wrapped her arms about his neck and sobbed into his black fur.

"What will I do?" she cried. "I want you to come back, Jaeger. I need you. I can't do this alone."

He rubbed his cheek against hers, his heart gripped with agony. She needed help, more help than he could give her, but he was not about to risk the world of man again. He knew what he needed to do, and it brought him nothing but more heartache.

She sat back, sniffing, and wiped the tears from her face. She drew a deep breath and tossed her hair back in defiance. "All right," she said quietly. "Enough of this self-pity. I haven't even asked you how you're feeling. The wound, did it heal?"

Jaeger nodded, though the injury still burned. He only wished his heart didn't ache as much. Rhiannon surveyed their surroundings, then got stiffly to her feet.

"Well, it looks like the caves will be home for a bit longer," she said, all traces of her tears gone. "You'll have to forgive my emotions, Jaeger. Carrying a child does this to a woman." She turned away but stopped when he gripped her skirt in his teeth. She looked down at him. "What? Are you in pain? Do you need to rest?"

He dropped the cloth, shook his head, then looked over his shoulder at what he hoped was another chance at civilization. Rhiannon seemed to catch his meaning at once. She shook her head.

"No, thank you! I'll not be walking up to another house real soon. I think I prefer the caves."

Jaeger shook his head again. No! Cold, dark caves are not the place for a woman carrying a child. You need your clan, Rhiannon, please. You need your clan. He rose, wincing in pain, and took a few steps away from her.

She frowned. "What? I don't understand."

"Don't you?"

The voice came from nowhere and everywhere. Darius stepped from behind a large boulder. Rhiannon gave a small, startled cry and darted to Jaeger's side. Jaeger glared at the Vector, hatred burning a hole in his gut. Darius regarded him thoughtfully, almost sadly, then turned his attention to Rhiannon.

"He no longer wishes you to be with him," he told her.

Rhiannon drew herself up rigidly. "I don't believe that. He just risked his life for me."

"Again," Darius said wryly.

Rhiannon frowned. "Yes, again."

Darius sighed, shaking his head. "And how many more times will he risk his life for yours? How many more brushes with death will he suffer to keep you safe?"

Jaeger let out a low growl, not understanding--or liking--the tone of Darius' voice. The Vector ignored him. Jaeger glanced up at Rhiannon, saw the uncertainty begin to grow in her eyes. He pressed up against her leg, hoping she would understand he was caring for her of his own choice.

"I...I don't mean to cause him to suffer," she stammered.

"Yet, he does suffer." Darius shrugged, gesturing at Jaeger. "Look at him. A man trapped inside the body of an animal, having to answer to animal instincts while at the same time possessing human intellect, human needs, human wants and desires. How do you think this is affecting him?"

Jaeger growled again, irritated that Darius was discussing him as if he could no longer understand human speech. Rhiannon's gaze was locked on him, though she seemed to be looking more through him than at him.

"But you did this to him!" she cried.

"I had no choice. He attacked another Vector, he defied the Sovereign, he took you away from your rightful master." Darius paused. "If you truly loved him, you would let him go."

"Go?" she echoed softly.

Jaeger's anger erupted. He darted between Rhiannon and Darius, growling, his eyes narrowed to slits as he glared up at the Vector.

Darius finally acknowledged him. "You're in pain," he said softly. "A wound from an arrow. I can tell you right now, Jaeger, it won't heal like you think it will. You no longer have that ability. Already, infection is setting in. In two weeks time, you'll most likely be dead."

"No!" Rhiannon cried. She dropped down beside Jaeger and gathered him close. "That's not true. It can't be! Jaeger, it's not true, is it?"

Jaeger remained still. Darius had only confirmed what he had already begun to suspect. Though the bleeding had stopped, whatever filth had coated the arrow had embedded itself deep within Jaeger's muscle. Walking had only sent it deeper. It was apparent now that Jaeger would not be able to rely on his Vector strength or magic to assist in the healing.

"No," Rhiannon said again and broke into sobs.

After a moment, Darius spoke again. "I can help you both."

"How?" Rhiannon lifted her tearstained face to him.

"I make you an offer. I will return Jaeger to his Vector form so that he can heal properly. Even so, it will take weeks to repair the damage. You will come with me and take your place beside Celd."

Horror swelled in Jaeger's chest. He whipped his head up to stare at Darius. *No!* his mind screamed, but all that came from his throat was a pitiful yowl of denial. He spun to look at Rhiannon. She was ashen-faced.

"If I do this," she whispered, "Jaeger will live?"

No! Jaeger screamed again and rested one paw on her arm.

"Yes, he will live," Darius replied.

Rhiannon looked into Jaeger's eyes, her hands gently stroking his fur.

Slowly, she nodded, then leaned forward to kiss him.

"I love you, Jaeger," she breathed. "Don't forget me."

Jaeger lifted his other paw to wrap both about her in an effort to keep her with him but Darius' magic claimed her, leaving Jaeger sprawled on the hard ground, alone.

Chapter Sixteen

Jaeger paced the cave, his mountain cat steps fast and furious, though still hampered by a slight limp. It had been almost two months since Rhiannon had disappeared, since Darius had returned him to his Vector form. Or at least a semblance of it. By night he was a Vector, able to shapeshift, filled with more-than-human strength, hungering for blood. But by day, he was still a mountain cat, driven by animal instinct alone. In the animal shape, he was mortal, vulnerable to being severely injured, crippled, even killed. He pushed the thought aside as rage consumed him for this foul trick Darius had played on him. He wanted to find the Vector as badly as he wanted to find Rhiannon.

He had not been able to find her, though not for lack of trying. He exhausted himself trying. He investigated every scent of blood, every rumor of a Vector or a witch's presence in every village he encountered in his travels. The only answer he could come up with was that Darius had returned Rhiannon to the Lair. And if she was there...

He sank down in despair. If she were in the Lair, there would be no saving her. He could not get back inside. He had been banished, doomed to wander in solitude for eternity, his familiar companion, despair, following him. Thoughts of the raging river in the canyon were coming all too frequently.

However, along with despair came a rage he had never experienced. It burned within, drove him, colored his nights, marred his days. Rage helped him drive away thoughts of the eternal peace that lay at the bottom of the river.

He lifted his head and looked outside the cave. It was night. Time for him to shift into Vector form. Then, by choice, he would immediately return to his animal form. What irony: He had yearned to be a man again, and now that he could be, he made a conscious choice not to. However, as an animal he could cover more ground, investigate rumors more thoroughly. It was not without its risks, of course. At the moment, he was close to a large village consisting mostly of hunters and trappers. Hunting parties were thick about the woods; and they didn't seem to care what their prey was. He walked outside, sniffing the cool air, even as the change took place.

He could smell blood. His thirst for the red liquid had not abated. In fact, it seemed to be intensifying. Even the kills he made while in animal form could not satisfy his yearnings. He wanted, needed, human blood. And he took it, no longer chastising himself for what he needed. A change had come over him; and when he fed, he did so with an anger and force previously unknown to him.

He lifted his head as the wind suddenly changed direction. A familiar scent wrapped around him. He frowned, puzzled, then changed into an owl. He took flight, winging silently over the dark countryside, his keen eyesight missing nothing. First, he needed to satisfy his hunger. Several field mice and a small hare took care of that. Then, he turned toward the nearby village and the source of the puzzling scent.

He fluttered to the top of a silo and scanned the ground below. There seemed to be a great deal of activity taking place near the town square. He flew closer, settling on the peaked roof of the church. A sizeable crowd, bearing torches and an assortment of weapons, was pushing and shoving toward the center of the open space. Their voices made clear they were aroused to a fever pitch. Jaeger tuned an ear to what they were saying.

"Get the rope!"

"We'll not have their kind in our town!"

"Hangin's not good enough for the likes of him!"

Jaeger watched as someone threw a thick rope over a protruding beam in front of a two-story inn. The crowd jostled and made way as a small knot of men emerged, dragging a young man toward the makeshift gallows. He was fighting them, struggling to free himself of both their hold and the tight ropes binding his wrists behind him. Even by torchlight, Jaeger could see he was ashen-faced with terror.

"Witch!" someone yelled.

The townsfolk quickly took up the chant. It seared into Jaeger's heart, quickened his pulse, sent him into a wild fury. Witch! So, that was the game, then! Jaeger swooped down from his perch, landing easily on the ground in the dark of a side street beside the tavern. He changed into a mountain cat and crept forward until he could see around the corner of the building.

The young man was now under the rope but the men holding him were having a hard time getting the noose about his neck. He ducked first one way, then the other, all the while screaming his innocence. Finally, one of his captors cuffed him soundly. He sagged toward the ground, and in that same moment, Jaeger sprang to land beside him.

The mob fell back with a gasp of shock and alarm, while their prey collapsed, dazed. Jaeger bared his teeth and let out a roar that echoed against the wooden buildings lining the square.

"It's the witch's familiar!" someone shouted.

"Kill it!" another screamed.

No one moved. Jaeger let out another angry yowl as the condemned man managed to regain his feet. He seemed just as terrified of Jaeger as the villagers were.

"It--it's not mine," he stammered, backing away.

Jaeger gave him a quick glare, then returned his attention to the crowd. Another growl erupted from his throat, and he took a step forward. The crowd fell back in response. Then, one of the braver men loosed an arrow. It was badly off-target and landed with a dull thud far to one side. Still, it was enough to both incite the crowd and to rouse Jaeger's ire even further.

Several dozen men pressed forward, shouting for the creature's death. Jaeger refused to back down. Instead, he again shapeshifted, this time into a shaggy brown bear, driving the crowd to a wild panic. As he stood up on his hind legs, he loosed yet another roar.

"Kill the witch, and his familiar dies as well!" a man shouted.

Another arrow soared through the air, followed by a dagger, both of which missed the young man by only inches. Blue eyes wide, his face almost as white as the moon, he stumbled and sought protection behind Jaeger.

"Come on! We can take him!"

"Kill the witch!"

The words rang out over the square, and the men rushed forward as one, circling Jaeger in an attempt to reach the young man. More arrows flew, and Jaeger heard the man cry out in pain. Rage boiled into fury; and in a split second, the bear transformed into a dragon.

Jaeger threw back his head and unleashed a stream of flame that arched madly into the night sky. This time the crowd had had enough. They threw down their weapons and fled, their terrified shrieks echoing shrilly. Jaeger turned his head toward the young man, then caught him up in one powerful forelimb. With just two hard beats of his wings, Jaeger lifted from the ground and shot up into the dark.

The young man lay limp in his grasp, bleeding heavily from an arrow embedded deep in his shoulder. The scent of iron-rich blood filled Jaeger's senses, sent his heart racing. He soared toward the cave he had called home for too many nights to remember.

He landed sure of foot, easing the young man to the cold stone floor, then once more assumed his Vector form. The man stared up at him through eyes glassy with pain.

"A Vector," he breathed, though he did not try to move away.

Jaeger hunkered down beside him to examine the wound and grimaced. Without a word, he pulled the quarrel free. The young man gasped; his body convulsed in agony and his eyes fluttered closed. For a moment, Jaeger could only watch the red blood spill out, soaking through the man's shirt, dripping to the floor. Tentatively, he touched the blood with one finger, then brought it to his mouth. Iron. Pure, strong, rich. The taste was familiar, and Jaeger's thoughts spun instantly to Rhiannon.

The young man looked a great deal like her, with his dark hair, fair skin, and blue eyes. Perhaps... Jaeger shook his head, not daring to allow himself the thought. He drew his pack forward and attempted to stop the bleeding. The wound, however, continued to pump blood no matter how long Jaeger pressed on the site.

Perplexed, he sat back to consider. He could give some of his own blood to the young man. It would stop the bleeding, true, but there was also a question if the man would cross over, would become one of the Vectors. Jaeger didn't know if he could do that to another--to plunge an innocent person into his own personal hell. Yet, if he didn't, the man would bleed to death. And what right did Jaeger have to allow that? Again, his pathetic lack of knowledge for his own kind came surging forward. How much blood was enough? How much was too much? Was there a certain amount that would heal, but not harm? He drew a deep breath, and before he could change his mind, he quickly bit into his own wrist. Blood, hot and red, spilled forth. Jaeger held his arm over the man's wound, allowing his blood to drip into it. Almost at once, the hemorrhage slowed, then stopped. The man shuddered several times, gasping as if in pain.

Jaeger drew his arm away, letting his own wound heal, then watched as the hole created by the arrow closed, the skin and tissue regenerating. It amazed him how the blood of a Vector affected a human. It was almost as profound as the way the blood of a human affected a Vector.

The young man opened his eyes, blinking slowly as he gazed up at Jaeger. "Please," he managed, lifting one hand.

Annoyance raced through Jaeger. "I have just saved your life," he said. "You've no need to beg for mercy from me."

"No," the man rasped, gripping Jaeger's arm with as much force as he could. "I...need...your help."

"And I have given it," Jaeger returned. "Your wound has healed. You will live. What more do you need?"

Tears sparked the young man's blue eyes, reminding Jaeger of Rhiannon once again. Pain tore through his heart, and he made to pull away from the man.

"No," the man said again, his voice barely above a whisper. "I need to...be bled."

Jaeger started. "Bled?" he breathed.

"Please. Magic...it's...too much..."

Jaeger understood at once. The man *was* a witch! Had used magic trying to escape his tormentors. Now, his blood was thick with iron. Iron that was killing him more rapidly than even the arrow wound had threatened to do. Jaeger frowned, looking at the amount of blood the man had already lost, wondering why it had not been enough.

The man's tears spilled over, ran down the sides of his face, yet still he maintained his grip on Jaeger's arm. "Please," he said again.

Jaeger complied.

The young man woke several hours later. He sat up with a cry of alarm, then sagged back to the ground once he registered his surroundings. Jaeger was surprised that he actually seemed relieved to find himself in a cold, gray cave with only a Vector for company.

"My thanks," the man murmured. "You risked a great deal to help me."

Jaeger shrugged. "Would you like some tea?"

The man peered over at him. "You drink tea?"

Jaeger couldn't help but smile. "I like to vary my diet."

The man reddened. "I'm sorry. I...I didn't--"

Jaeger interrupted him with a wave of his hand. "That's all right. Come, have something to eat."

The man didn't even try to rise. Instead, he simply scooted himself closer to the fire and the food. "That looks like rabbit."

"It is. Help yourself."

The man took a chunk of the meat, tasted it, then raised his eyebrows in surprise. Apparently, he didn't believe Vectors were good for anything but taking blood.

"By the way," he said around a mouthful of meat, "my name is Vail."

"Jaeger." He paused. "You look like you might be clan."

"I am."

"Then your people are close by as well?"

Vail glanced at him, then shook his head. "No. Actually, I'm on my own."

"I see. And you are a witch?"

"Yes."

"What were you doing in the village? And using magic?"

Vail sagged. "I...I'm looking for my sister."

"Your sister?" Jaeger sat up straighter, his heart beginning to pound. "Her name?"

"Rhiannon." Vail's shoulder's sagged further, as if merely saying the name smothered him in grief.

Jaeger stared at him, astonished. "Rhiannon?" he whispered.

"Yes. She disappeared months ago. I guess continuing to search is--" He stopped suddenly, his mouth gaping, his gaze fixed on Jaeger. "Wait! You might know! She went looking for a Vector! She said she sensed the presence of one not far from our camp. But she never came back! Could you...would you even...?" He broke off again, his eyes pleading.

The words reminded Jaeger of the pain he had felt when Rhiannon had told him of her search. Of how she had tracked him--or Celd. A Vector to help her with her illness, a partnership, a business arrangement. It hurt as much now as it had then, despite Rhiannon's claims of love for him. He took a sip of his tea and regarded Vail.

"I knew Rhiannon," he said softly.

"What?" The word barely escaped Vail's lips. His face, already pale, went even more so. "Knew? Then she's...you..."

Anger flitted through Jaeger at what the man was suggesting. "No, I did not kill her," he snapped. "I found her, badly beaten and bleeding from a self-inflicted wound. I helped her, Vail. I did not kill her."

Vail drew back from Jaeger's anger. "My apologies," he mumbled. "I thank you for helping her. I knew no good could come of her going off on her own."

Jaeger paused a moment. "She had been raped by four men."

Vail went white, then passed one hand over his face.

When he said nothing more, Jaeger continued. "This does not upset you?"

Vail sighed. "What good will it do to condemn dead men?"

"Dead men?"

The young man nodded. "If any man dared to touch my sister in that way, he paid with his life. I know her."

The words brought Jaeger up short. He had never thought Rhiannon capable of killing. He wondered why she had not used her magic against the farmer who had attacked her. Perhaps carrying a child prevented it.

Vail shuddered. "She had such high hopes," he murmured.

"What do you mean?"

He looked up at Jaeger, his blue eyes shiny with tears. "My clan...all of us...we're Bleeders. It's something in our history, our families through time. We try to bleed ourselves, of course, but all too often it ends in death from infection or blood loss. We discovered there is something in a Vector's bite that helps slow the formation of iron in our bodies. It's as if the bite cleanses our blood, removing the iron like no simple bleeding can do. That's why, even though I bled a great deal from my wound, I still had far too much iron in my body. I needed whatever it is a Vector has to offer. Rhiannon knew all of this. She came up with the idea that perhaps Vectors could help us. And we could help them in return. We could provide the blood they need to survive. Our payment would be life as well."

"She wanted to present your entire clan to the Vectors?"

Vail nodded, dropping his piece of meat back into the fire. "It sounded like an equitable partnership. Only, she never returned. I've been searching for her ever since. Please, Jaeger, if you know where she is, tell me. I only want to take her home."

Jaeger studied him for a long moment, then averted his gaze. "I wish I knew where she was, Vail. I wish I knew."

Chapter Seventeen

Jaeger peered over Vail's shoulder, carefully watching the water in the cup the young witch held. He saw nothing on the still surface but Vail's reflection.

"Will this work?" he asked, not for the first time.

Vail sighed, shooting him a quick, irritated glance. "I told you, I don't know. I'll do my best. But if Rhiannon is in the Vector Lair, I might not be able to reach her at all."

Jaeger sighed and began to pace. Vail had agreed to attempt to scrye for Rhiannon using his magic. He had not been successful up to this point but was now hoping to draw on Jaeger's magic to supplement his own. Jaeger hadn't told Vail that he now had Vector blood, and quite possibly Vector magic of his own.

"There!" Vail suddenly cried. "Look!"

Jaeger darted to his side and peered into the cup. A blurry image was beginning to form. "Is it her?" he whispered, half-afraid that his voice would cause the image to disappear.

Vail was quiet, directing more magic at the water. The image quieted, cleared; and Jaeger gasped.

Rhiannon!

"Where is she?" he breathed.

"She...she's with child," Vail stammered. "Those men...the ones who raped her...they--"

"No!" Jaeger said at once. "No, it was not the men who raped her. Be assured of that."

"Then, who?"

Jaeger refused to answer. "Where is she?" he asked.

"I...I don't know. Do you recognize anything?"

Jaeger peered closer. "It looks almost like a cave, like this one. But I don't know why she would be there."

Vail was quiet, his brow furrowed in thought. "Let me see if I can back up a bit on the image. Maybe I can get a wider angle."

Jaeger nodded, though he would have preferred to get closer. He wanted to see Rhiannon up close, see if she was all right. He didn't trust Celd in the slightest. Rhiannon was a feisty woman, with a strength Celd might find not only intimidating but also challenging. It would not be above the Vector to beat Rhiannon into submission, to force her with ways other than magic to do his bidding. The mere thought of Celd laying a brutal hand on Rhiannon sent fury through Jaeger.

"It *is* a cave!" Vail cried, interrupting Jaeger's thoughts. "But not in the Grottos. It looks like it's somewhere near the ocean."

"The ocean?" Jaeger was truly astonished to hear that. Vectors tried to avoid the ocean--there was something about the salt water...he wasn't exactly sure what it was, but he had been severely warned by both his mother and his father. He was to stay away from any source of dangerous water, but most definitely the ocean. He had always taken that warning to heart.

Now, here, apparently, was Celd, holed up in a cave right on the edge of the sea itself. It didn't make sense. He nudged Vail.

"Is there any way to find out where she is? I mean, *where* along the ocean?"

"Well, I could draw back even further, maybe get a few landmarks, but I could also lose the vision altogether."

Jaeger hesitated. He desperately wanted to see Rhiannon closer, but he also wanted to find out her location. He supposed seeing how she was would be irrelevant, if he couldn't find her at all. He nodded. "Then back off. Let's see if we can pinpoint the area."

Vail did as requested, but still nothing looked familiar to Jaeger. He scanned the landscape as it rolled past, taking note of anything that he might be able to use in his search. Finally, the vision wavered and disappeared. Vail sat back with a heavy sigh.

"I'm sorry," he mumbled, rubbing at his temples.

Jaeger laid one hand on the young man's shoulder. "You did well. For the first time, I have direction. We will find your sister, Vail. I promise you that."

"How?" Vail asked, looking up at him. "You can't go outside in the daylight, can you?"

Jaeger hesitated. "I can, but not as a man. And at night, I can transform into any number of creatures."

Vail gave a small smile. "Yes, I noticed. What a wondrous power that must be. Would that I had such a gift. I could have easily escaped those men."

Jaeger regarded him thoughtfully. "But you did try. You used your magic."

Vail grimaced, the smile fading. "I did. But the magic I have is very weak. Not like Rhiannon's. She has a true gift. Still, even she is at the beginning of a long journey of learning. It seems our lives are over before we really learn all that we are capable of." He sighed. "It's too bad we couldn't find a way to extend that life, to really learn our craft."

"And if you could? What would you do with your talent?"

Vail looked at him. "Help people, of course. We could be healers of the greatest kind. People wouldn't have to die of disease and infection. We could stop that. We could stop people from falling victim to road bandits as well. We could enhance crops, so people would no longer starve, purify water so no one died of thirst. We could make the world a better place."

Jaeger thought a moment. "But, first, you would have to be accepted. It seems to me people fear those with such a gift, rather than embrace them."

"'Tis true, sadly true. But, if we had more power, we could also protect ourselves against the results of such fear."

"But there is always the possibility such power would breed tyranny. Perhaps that is why people fear it."

It was Vail's turn to ponder. He nodded slowly. "It's a double-edged sword, isn't it? How do Vectors deal with it? How do you keep from using your incredible powers to control everything and everyone?"

Jaeger gave a short laugh. "I can only speak for myself, Vail. I do not wish to control anyone. I have a hard enough time merely controlling myself."

Vail shot him a sidelong glance. "In what respect?"

Jaeger was quiet a moment. "I have never bled a human to the point of death, Vail. In fact, I had never tasted human blood at all until just months past." He caught the look on Vail's face. "And, no, your sister was not the first, though, in some ways, it would ease my guilt if she had been. At least, she was looking to be bled."

"I sense no small amount of bitterness in that statement."

Irritation coursed through Jaeger. "Are you an empath as well?"

Vail hesitated. "Actually, I am."

The words startled Jaeger. He got to his feet, turning away from the young man. "What do you know of Vectors, Vail?"

"More than most. Both Rhiannon and I researched them before she left."

"Researched?" The word increased Jaeger's ire. "Then I was studied, like some animal in the field?"

"No, but we both thought it was wise to know as much as possible before we made our proposal to the Vectors."

Jaeger whirled on him. "Proposal! I loved her, Vail! I love her still! Yet, her interest in me seemingly was purely one of business. How do you think that makes me feel? Use your empathic abilities to read that!"

Vail was quiet a moment, then he, got up and moved to stand in front of Jaeger. "Have you made love with my sister?"

The question startled Jaeger from his anger. He felt color rush to his cheeks, though why he couldn't say. "We...have been intimate, yes."

"Then there is your answer. Rhiannon has been with no man...that is, willingly. A rape she cannot be faulted for. If my sister lay with you, it was in love, not because of a business arrangement. Do not doubt that." He paused, as if unsure whether to voice his next thoughts. "And your love for her? How do you see that?"

Jaeger stared at him, clearly understanding the meaning. Darius had asked the same thing. His anger resurfaced. "Do you think I mistake lust for love?" he roared. "Yes, she was the first woman I lay with, but I believe I am capable of sorting out a physical need from an emotional one! If I were only seeking something physical, I could have it! With any number of people, any time I choose. I could make even you yearn for me, Vail. I could make you answer to me. I could make you satisfy the physical needs I have!"

He had drawn very close to the man in his ranting, and now reached out to grip Vail by the back of the neck. The man trembled, his gaze locked on Jaeger's. The Vector felt the sexual tension arc between them, and he trembled as well. For just a split second, he thought he might act on that tension, take both the young man's blood and his body. By force of will, he turned aside and stomped to the far side of the cave.

He heard Vail's breath rush from him as the young man collapsed to the stone floor. For several moments, there was only silence, then Jaeger sighed.

"I'm sorry," he mumbled. "This is all still quite new to me. I have only just begun to experience this...lust that comes with the Growth. But trust me in this--I love your sister with my heart, not my loins." When Vail said nothing, Jaeger looked over at him.

The young man had a distant look on his face, a furrow on his brow, as if musing over something extremely interesting and confusing.

Jaeger frowned. "What is it? What's wrong?"

Vail shook his head. "Nothing is wrong. I was...I was only thinking what a wonderful talent you have."

"Talent?" Jaeger shook his head, thoroughly confused.

Vail nodded as if in a daze. "The way you made me want you, ache for you. I would have given myself to you. Yet, I know my interest lies not in men, but in women. One in particular." A dreamy smile crossed his face. "Rachael," he breathed, as if he revered the name itself. "If I could make her ache so for me..."

Jaeger practically choked on his astonishment. He stared at Vail in open-mouthed wonder. He had used his Vector magic on the boy, almost coerced him into a sexual encounter, forced him to go against his own inclinations, and Vail was musing how to do the same thing to the woman of his dreams.

Vail abruptly lifted his gaze to Jaeger's, only now realizing the Vector's shock. The young man went red.

"Well, it's that--I--you see, I--" He broke off with a shrug. "I'm twenty-two and yet a virgin. Still, that doesn't mean that...well, that I don't have...desires. It's just that I only want to share those desires with Rachael. Now, if I could take just a little of what you just did, and..." He stopped, swallowed hard, and averted his gaze.

Jaeger abruptly felt laughter swelling up inside him. He thought he had been imparting an explanation, a lesson in love over lust. Yet, Vail had assimilated it quite differently. A chuckle escaped Jaeger, much to Vail's consternation.

Jaeger shook his head. "I guess I'm far older than I thought. At least mentally. At any rate, let's get some rest. Later, we go look for Rhiannon."

Chapter Eighteen

They left the caves at dawn, Jaeger in the form of the mountain cat. He had not yet explained to Vail that the changing was not of his own desires. He didn't see that it mattered. He had told Vail that he would not be able to converse, and so they walked in silence for several hours, each lost in his own thoughts. Then Vail spoke.

"That arrow I took," he began. "It was a nasty wound."

Jaeger nodded his black head.

Vail continued, flexing his shoulder. "You are a gifted healer. It feels like there was never an injury there."

Jaeger drew a quick breath. He still hadn't told Vail how he had healed the wound. He wasn't sure if he wanted to. Fortunately, Vail changed the subject.

"Back there, when you did whatever it was you did--well, you said you loved my sister but not with your loins. Does that mean, then, that your taste is not for women?"

Jaeger shot a quick glance at him, nodded, then shook his head, further confusing the answer. Vail seemed to take it in stride.

"The research I did with Rhiannon said that there is often a connection between the taking of blood and a sexual response. Not always, but often. Both seem to provide an orgasmic relief. So, does that mean that Vectors are attracted to men as well?"

A sneeze is an orgasmic relief, Jaeger wanted to scream, *but that doesn't mean I am attracted to noses.* He let out a soft growl, indicating his annoyance with the subject matter.

Vail looked down at him, then laughed. "I'm sorry. I'm prying."

Yes, you are, Jaeger wanted to reply. He had already experienced the sexual side of taking blood. Many times over in the last two months. He was as confused as anyone by his responses. He supposed if he had studied his Vector heritage a little more thoroughly, he would understand these things. Still, it seemed he was rapidly finding out despite his lack of formal schooling. He cringed as Vail once more began talking. He wondered if the boy was ever quiet.

"While we're traveling together, I would suppose you could make use of my blood. I know I could certainly use your help in that respect. I am a little concerned regarding the sexual side of it, however. I mean, not that--"

It was more than Jaeger could take, and he bounded away from the young man.

"Wait!" Vail called. "Was it something I said?"

Jaeger kept running, knowing he would not only have to face the boy's questions but his own, at some point. Maybe, if he could get a good kill, he could satisfy his blood-thirst. Then, perhaps, he could resist the blood Vail offered, even though he knew that wouldn't help Vail at all.

The area they traveled was rough terrain. Huge boulders were scattered about barren ground, looking as if the hand of God had dropped them. In between the gray rocks, scrub vied for space and whatever water was available deep underground. The whole area was a sea of subdued colors that looked as if the life had been drained out of them.

Jaeger ran until he spotted a large jackrabbit. The rabbit saw him at the same moment. Driven by the internal fears Vail's words had evoked, Jaeger made short work of the chase. This time he did not even stop to consider if the creature had young.

After devouring the rabbit, Jaeger debated on whether or not to return to Vail. For the first time, he was actually glad that he did not possess the ability to speak. Maybe Vail would get tired of talking if there was no response. With a sigh, Jaeger picked up the young man's trail, though he took his time rejoining him.

Vail had stopped to rest. He looked up at Jaeger, his eyes holding such relief and dismay, Jaeger hung his head in guilt. He sat down next to the young man.

"I'm sorry," Vail mumbled. "People tell me I talk too much. I guess that's true. But my mother used to tell me that's the only way people learn things. By asking questions. Course, she also used to tell me I should listen better."

Jaeger cocked his head at the boy, then laid one heavy black paw on the boy's arm.

Vail grinned. "Then I'm forgiven?"

Jaeger nodded and nudged him, indicating they should continue. He wanted to find shelter before nightfall. He was exhausted and needed to rest before continuing to the ocean, though how he would find Rhiannon in the vast expanse of beaches, he didn't know. When Vail sat still, Jaeger nudged him harder, knocking him off-balance. Vail grabbed out for a handhold and caught Jaeger round the neck, pulling him over as well. That simple action saved Vail's life.

An arrow ricocheted off the boulder, clattering harmlessly to the ground. Jaeger jerked his head up, his gaze darting over the rock-strewn landscape. Vail yelped and scrambled behind the boulder he had been leaning against. Jaeger darted away, cursing himself for his lack of attention. The wind shifted, and immediately Jaeger scented his quarry. He crouched low to the ground and crept stealthily, silently, forward. A moment later, he saw a small knot of mounted men, all armed with longbows. They had reloaded and were setting up to loose a volley of arrows in Vail's direction. Jaeger recognized them as men from the village, some of the same ones who had tried to hang Vail just days earlier.

Jaeger hesitated, glancing at the sun. It was well on its way down. If only he could buy time, he could use the coming darkness to shapeshift to something more powerful, something better able to deal with six well-built men and their lethal weapons. He crept closer, then started in astonishment. One of them was the farmer who had attacked Rhiannon. Anger swelled inside him, and a low growl escaped his throat. The six men turned as one.

"It's him!" the man cried. "That's the familiar that attacked my father! I knew it was the same one."

That's right. It's me. So, come and get me. He growled again, his gaze flicking over the men.

One of them raised his bow, leveling his arrow at Jaeger. The farmer stopped him. "No. This one is mine. Detrick, you come with me. You others, go for the witch."

The words sent hatred and rage burning through Jaeger. He spun and raced away, determined to keep the men away from Vail. The boy was still crouched behind the rock, and Jaeger felt the tingle of magic surrounding him. He would trust Vail to protect himself until night fell. Their gazes met briefly, then Jaeger yowled to draw the hunters' attention and tore across the rocky ground.

"There he goes!" Detrick shouted. "Come on!"

Jaeger raced through the sparse brush, dodging boulders and leaping over piles of loose rock. The two hunters followed, driving their horses with shouts and slaps. Even as he ran, Jaeger felt the daylight fading, shifting, the night calling to his Vector blood. He streaked onward, a dark shadow in the rapidly darkening evening. As he did so, he was aware that one of his pursuers was falling back, and he focused on the expectation that he would be cut off.

An arrow bit into the ground to his left, spattering up dirt and loose rock. Jaeger quickly turned away, hearing a hiss as another arrow flew over his back. He doubled back toward Vail. The young witch couldn't maintain the magic shields for long, and Jaeger needed to be close by when they finally failed and exposed Vail to the rest of the hunting party.

He was too late. Two men held Vail while the other two took turns pounding him with fists and heavy clubs. Vail was bleeding from numerous gashes and hung limply in the men's arms, too weak to fight back, even if he could.

Pure fury at the hunters' cowardice tore through Jaeger. As the sun disappeared below the horizon, he felt his magic surge alongside his rage. Between one step and the next, he shapeshifted into his dragon form. It didn't take but one roar to make the hunters scatter in terror.

Vail fell to his knees.

The farmer suddenly appeared, obviously having doubled back. He kicked his horse forward, leaning low in the saddle. As he thundered past Vail, he lashed out with his dagger, burying it in the lad's back. Jaeger's roar of disbelief mixed with Vail's cry of agony. The Vector unleashed a stream of fire, blocking the fleeing men's path.

They swerved to avoid the conflagration, but in their confusion ran straight toward Jaeger. He bore down on them, his need for vengeance overriding any compassion or leniency. His sharp foreclaws tore into their flesh, exposing bone and muscle, shredding skin, mangling limbs. When all but one joined the growing heap of tangled meat, he turned his rage on that one--the man who had attacked Rhiannon, hunted him down, and attempted to kill Vail.

The man backed away, his face twisted with terror. He held up both hands as if to shield himself. Jaeger drew back his great head and unleashed a stream of flame that completely engulfed the man. The man screamed, batted at his burning clothes and hair and turned to run. Jaeger watched as he stumbled, then fell, consumed by fire. His shrieks died with him. Jaeger roared his approval.

"Jaeger, help...please..."

Vail's thin voice broke through Jaeger's rage. He immediately returned to Vector form and rushed to the young man's side. Vail lay in a pool of blood, his face so swollen that his eyes were little more than dark slits in the bruised flesh. Blood saturated his clothes, wet the brown dirt beneath him, and matted his hair. Even so, he managed to lift one hand and grip Jaeger's arm.

"Rhiannon," he whispered. "You find her. Help her."

"We'll find her together, Vail. You will not die." He took up the pack, and then grimaced as he pulled the dagger free from Vail's back.

The young man let out a cry of agony and fainted. Quickly, without thought, Jaeger bit into his own flesh and once again allowed his blood to flow into Vail's wound. Satisfied it would heal, Jaeger returned to dragon form, plucked Vail's limp body from the ground and took to the air. He flew westward, toward the ocean, toward Rhiannon. He was exhausted, yet he was determined to put as much distance as he could between the village, and himself and Vail.

As he flew, he became ever more sickened by what he had just done. He had killed like that before, with the same overwhelming hatred and vengeance. The men in the alleyway were the first, these men the next. Would there be others? Somehow Jaeger thought there might be.

What would his dear mother say now? How could he ever reconcile his actions to her memory? How could he go on? Tears stung his eyes, burned into his cheeks, and were dried by the cool wind blowing against him.

He made a firm decision. He would find Rhiannon, and reunite her with her brother. Then, he would take them both to another land, far away, where they could live in peace, no longer persecuted for what they were. He would return to the Lair, let the Sovereign do whatever he desired. No punishment could hurt worse than living as the Vector he had become. Death seemed to be the only way out.

He found shelter just before dawn. It wasn't much, just an overhang on the side of a rocky hillside. Still, it provided some degree of protection from the searing sunlight. Despite his grievous wounds, Vail had regained consciousness. The Vector blood Jaeger had given him was healing his wounds slowly but steadily. Jaeger had thought to give him more, but had decided against it. He still wasn't sure what effect the amount of blood he had given the young man would do to him. Vail seemed quite surprised he was not dead and kept reaching to his back in search of the wound he thought should be there.

Jaeger watched him across the small fire, knowing he should explain. He was just not sure how to approach it. In the end, Vail saved him the trouble.

"What sort of magic did you use on me?" he asked softly. "How is it I can take such a beating and a stabbing, and yet survive?"

"Because I have given you some of my blood," Jaeger replied bluntly. "The arrow you took in the village hit one of your main blood vessels. You were bleeding to death. Be angry with me if you will, but, at the time, it was the only thing I could think of to do that would keep you alive. I gave you more to heal the stab wound."

Vail stared at him, his blue eyes holding a myriad of emotions.

Jaeger glanced toward the mouth of the overhang. "If you wish to take vengeance on me, you will soon have your chance. At dawn, I will once again change into the mountain cat. I have no choice. It is my punishment for attacking one of the Chosen. I am most vulnerable while in animal form. You may kill me any number of ways. You can also kill me in Vector form, by drowning, burning, poisoning or by impaling me with an oaken stake."

"Why are you telling me this?" Vail murmured.

Jaeger rubbed wearily at his face. "I don't know. Maybe because I look forward to my own death these days. I don't know who I am anymore. I am not proud of the things I have done in the past few months, of what I have become. And I am sorry for pulling you onto this road with me."

Vail drew a deep breath, then shook his head. "There is no need to apologize, Jaeger. I am grateful for your help. I am alive. To me, that sounds a lot better than being dead."

Jaeger studied him for a long moment. It was such a simple statement, yet profound in its depth. He managed a small smile, then got up.

"I must shift," he said quietly, wondering at his next words. "I would prefer it be done in private. I will be back in a moment. I suggest we spend the day resting. We've a long journey ahead of us."

Vail nodded, lay back, and closed his eyes. Jaeger watched him a moment longer, then stepped into the cool darkness of a nearby cleft in the rock to allow the shift.

Chapter Nineteen

They spent the next nine days walking during the night and resting during the day. In all of that time, Jaeger managed to satisfy his cravings by feasting on animals procured during his hunts. Vail benefited from those kills as well, since Jaeger would always make sure to bring some meat back to whatever form of shelter the two of them had managed to find. Still, Jaeger could see the fatigue on the young man's face, hear it in his voice. And he could smell the iron. It got stronger with each passing day. Vail needed to be bled, but neither one of them seemed able to face that.

Finally, on the tenth day, just after dusk, when Jaeger had once more reclaimed his Vector body, Vail turned to him.

"I can't go on," he said softy. "Not like this. I don't know how to ask this of you, Jaeger, other than by being blunt. I need to be bled. If you do not wish to do it, I can attempt a simple bleeding on my own. It won't be as effective or last as long, but..." He shrugged.

Jaeger grimaced, turning away from him. "I can do as you ask," he said. "I can promise you relief from your ailment. What I can't promise you is that we won't be affected. You now have Vector blood in your system as well. Apparently, not enough to cure your ailment, but enough that it might change our emotional reactions to a blood sharing. We may experience a sexual response as well. Are you going to be able to handle that?"

Vail was quiet, and Jaeger turned, expecting to see the young man's face screwed up in disgust. Instead, he saw tears glistening in the blue eyes. Tears that spilled over and ran in silver streaks down Vail's pale cheeks. In that moment, Jaeger saw Rhiannon, and his heart cried out for her.

They were close to the beach, so close. Jaeger knew that Vail would be devastated if he could not continue. He sighed and approached the young man slowly. With trembling hand, he reached up to brush aside the tears.

"I will help you, Vail," he said quietly. "But first, let me satisfy my hunger on a wild animal. I just don't want to..." He stopped, not sure exactly what he wanted to say.

Vail nodded and sagged to the floor. "Do what you must. I'll be waiting for you." He lay down on the dirt of the small cave they had found and curled into a fetal position.

Jaeger eyed him with concern. "Take care of the fire," he finally said. "I'll bring back some dinner as well."

Vail made no response, and Jaeger quickly moved outside the cave. Once there, he shifted into a great horned owl. He wanted to waste no time with the hunt tonight. He needed something fast and easy. He had seen a proliferation of jackrabbits during his earlier hunts, and now sought them out. It didn't take him more than an hour to bring down two fat specimens. One he ate immediately, more to satisfy his need for blood than to relieve his hunger. The other he took back to the shelter.

He shifted to Vector form while still outside. He knew it was silly--Vail had already seen him shapechange several times--yet he felt that his privacy had been violated when he changed in front of the young man. He quickly cleaned the rabbit and stepped into the cave.

"Vail?" he called softly, approaching the fire.

The young man woke with a startled gasp. "Oh," he murmured. "It's you. You're back."

"And I brought dinner." Jaeger dropped down by the fire, skewered the rabbit carcass on a heavy stick and set it to roast. He turned his gaze on Vail.

The boy was pale, shivering; yet, his face was shiny with perspiration. Jaeger frowned, moving closer to him. The scent of iron was almost overwhelming, reminding Jaeger of the first time he had scented Rhiannon. As siblings, the two carried the same smell, the same mixture of iron and fragrance, though Vail's lacked the exotic sweet quality that Rhiannon's held. He drew a deep breath, barely conscious of his actions.

Vail let out a heavy sigh and leaned against Jaeger's shoulder, as if too fatigued to sit up on his own. Alarmed, Jaeger put one arm about the boy to support him. He could tell by Vail's trembling that he had already waited too long. He pulled the young man close in a tight embrace, closed his eyes, and bit.

The first taste was almost more than he could handle. It rushed into him, filled his senses, brought every nerve within him alive. His body responded so quickly it left his mind reeling, his skin tingling, his desires teetering on the threshold of ecstasy. When Vail unexpectedly grabbed his shirt in a desperate hold, it pushed him over that threshold.

They fell to the ground, Jaeger atop Vail, his incisors still embedded in the young man's neck. Vail moaned, writhing beneath him, his grip on

Jaeger's arms erasing any hope of separation. Jaeger felt every inch of Vail's lean wiry body, heard his breathing as it came in short gasps, smelled the increase in iron as Vail's passion increased. Jaeger trembled, trying in vain to control his wild emotions, trying in vain to separate the bloodletting from the sexual response. Then the unexpected happened.

Vail used what little magic he possessed, enhanced by the Vector blood he now carried. The magic swirled around Jaeger, seized him, commanded him. His yearning for Vail spiraled out of control; his rationality clouded by the spell Vail created. He could not pull back, could not thwart it. When Vail abruptly cried out in orgasmic release, Jaeger joined him, riding the waves of ecstasy that swelled through his mind.

For a short time, the only sounds in the cave were the sizzling of the meat over the fire and the two men's soft gasps. Then Jaeger pulled away from Vail and sat up, guilt once more his companion. He heard Vail move though the young man said nothing. The silence pressed against Jaeger like a living thing, threatening to suffocate him. He surged to his feet and strode to the cave entrance.

"Wait!" Vail's call was soft yet insistent.

Jaeger stopped but did not turn around. He stood, his back stiff, his hands clenched at his sides. All he wanted to do was escape, to run from this humiliation, this guilt. He started violently when he felt Vail's hand on his shoulder. The touch burned him, and he whirled, backing away, shocked to see the small grin on the young man's face.

"I would still love to learn how you do that," Vail said quietly.

The words, coupled with Jaeger's highly-strung emotions, were too much. A chuckle escaped him, a chuckle that turned to laughter. It echoed in the small cave, bouncing from wall to wall, floor to ceiling. It surrounded Jaeger, engulfed him, left him breathless and thanking the gods overhead for bringing both Rhiannon and her brother into his life.

He draped an arm about Vail's shoulders and walked him back to the fire. "You know, you appear to have quite a good grasp of the concept," he told the young man. "That reaction wasn't all my doing. Sit down. Eat. It's probably burned by now."

Vail plucked the roasted hare from the fire and examined it. "No, it's fine. Have you eaten?"

Jaeger started, then again burst into laughter. Vail seemed surprised, then realized what he had asked. He, too, began to laugh, though he flushed with embarrassment. He pulled some meat from the spit and chewed it thoughtfully. After a moment, he spoke.

"So, do you think I know enough about this to use it on Rachael?"

Jaeger grinned and shook his head. "Most likely. But you may find that she will come to you of her own volition. And you may prefer that in the long run."

Vail thought on the words. "I suppose that would be better. Then I wouldn't have to always be thinking that she came to me only because of magic." He took another few bites, then again looked at Jaeger. "Will we travel tonight? I feel quite well enough now. And I really want to find Rhiannon."

In truth, Jaeger was just as anxious, but he didn't want to push Vail to the point of such profound fatigue again. He wasn't sure if either of them could handle another such explosive encounter. "We'll walk for a while, maybe not all night. You need your rest."

Vail tossed him a sly, teasing glance. "So do you."

It was Jaeger's turn to blush. He rose, brushing the dust from his clothing. "Let's go. I think you're quite recovered. At the least, your tongue and wit are."

Vail grinned, finished off the meat, and followed. He scuffed out the fire and picked up the pack.

Jaeger took it from him. "Let me carry it. You've done your share."

"If you insist."

The two men left the cave together, both determined to find Rhiannon for different reasons.

It took the pair another two weeks to reach the ocean. During that time, Jaeger became more relaxed about accepting the gift of blood that Vail offered. In addition, Vail grew better able to control his emotional demands when Jaeger fed, which vastly relieved Jaeger's guilt.

Their first view of the ocean came just before daybreak. A full moon rode low in a black sky, casting soft white light over land and sea. Jaeger stood atop a knoll, his eyes wide with wonder at the stunning scene before him.

The ocean stretched forever, a velvet coverlet spread beneath a diamond-studded canopy. A cool breeze drifted inland, bringing with it the scent of salt. It touched lightly at Jaeger's hair, wrapped seductively about his neck, kissed his cheeks with moisture. He couldn't understand why his parents had warned him away from it. It seemed safe enough.

He glanced sideways at Vail. "Well, do we continue? Or do you want to stop and rest?"

Vail drew a deep breath, his gaze also on the ocean. "I want to find my sister," he said softly. "But..."

"But?"

Vail turned to him. "Who's with my sister?" he asked. "I know someone is, someone you don't care for. Yet, you have not spoken of this person. Why?"

Jaeger paused. "Let's find someplace for a fire and a meal. We can talk.

First, I need to hunt. You're hungry, aren't you?"

"No, not really. I saved quite a bit of meat from that rabbit you brought down earlier today. Although," he said with a grimace, "I am getting a little tired of rabbit."

Jaeger chuckled. "It's the most abundant game out here, and the easiest to catch. I don't want to go raiding some poor farmer's livestock. Now, I suppose, with all that water out there, we can add fish to our diet. I don't know what else the ocean provides."

"Lots," Vail answered as they began walking. "Crabs, shrimp, clams, all sorts of fish, and seagrass."

"Really? All of that? Then you've been to the sea before?"

"Yes, further south. My clan lived on the beach for a summer. It was wonderful. We worked hard but it didn't seem like work at all. At night, we would light huge fires of driftwood, then sing and dance until all hours. In fact, that's where I first fell in love with Rachael. Watching her dance is like watching an angel in heaven."

Jaeger lifted his eyebrows, amused at the dreamy way Vail always spoke of Rachael. He supposed it was not unlike how he sounded when he spoke of Rhiannon. Two love-struck men yearning to be in their lovers' arms once again. Jaeger sighed. He wondered if that would ever happen.

"There." He pointed to a rocky overhang facing the ocean. "We can stop there and rest. We need to plan our approach. If you're up to it, I'd like you to scrye again. I want to get a better picture of where Rhiannon is."

"I can do that."

They trudged to the overhang and crawled beneath it. In minutes, Jaeger had started a small fire. He took a cup from his pack, filled it with water, and handed it to Vail. The young man settled with his back against the rock and began to work his magic. He peered into the water, waiting for the images to appear. Jaeger replaced the waterskin in the pack and slid beside him.

When at last the shapes began to form on the surface of the water, Jaeger was stunned. He could see Rhiannon very clearly. She lay on her side, her face visible. She was pale, her eyes half closed in either fatigue or illness. Instinctively, Jaeger reached out one hand toward her, then drew back.

Vail said nothing but pulled back on the image, widening it. Now, Jaeger could see Rhiannon's pregnant abdomen. She was caressing it lightly, as if in pain. Even as he watched, she grimaced, her eyes squeezing shut, her mouth forming a tight line.

"She's in labor!" Vail gasped

"No," Jaeger murmured. "It's too soon. She's not far enough into the pregnancy."

Vail shot him a quick glance. "The baby seems to think so."

True alarm rushed through Jaeger. "Widen the image. I need to see Celd."

"Who is Celd?"

"The...father of her child."

"Celd?" Again Vail looked up at him. "But I thought that you... I mean..."

Jaeger averted his gaze. "No. I wish it was me, but it is Celd."

"And this Celd is who?"

"Please!" Jaeger snapped. "Enough questions! Widen the image!"

The boy started, alarm registering in his blue eyes. The image in the water blurred and faded.

"No!" Jaeger roared. "Bring it back!"

"I--I can't," Vail cried. He tossed the cup to the ground and scampered out of Jaeger's way.

Jaeger stared at him. Anger, fear, guilt--they all tore into his senses, confusing and frightening him. He whirled away from Vail to lean against the stone, hiding his face and his fears.

"Who is Celd?" Vail asked again, his voice soft.

"I," said another voice, "am Celd."

Jaeger whirled as wicked pain shot through him. He doubled over, his breath hissing outward. Celd glared at him, while Vail pressed back against the rocky wall, his face white.

"Where is she?" Celd demanded.

"What?" Jaeger managed, then gasped as more pain seared through him. A second later, something soothing wrapped around him, driving back the dizzying pain. His gaze shot to Vail, then back to Celd.

The Vector seemed not to notice Vail's interference. His anger at Jaeger commanded his attention.

"I asked you a question!" he spat.

"I...I thought she was with you." Jaeger maintained his position, allowing Celd to think he was still gripped in pain. He wasn't about to alert the Vector to what Vail was doing.

"If she was with me, would I be here?" Celd bellowed.

"But, Darius--"

"Darius!" Celd interrupted, surprise on his face. "When did you speak with Darius?"

Jaeger shook his head, not really sure how long ago it had been. "He found me. He was sent to dispense my...punishment for attacking you. He did so. He also took Rhiannon away with him. He said he was taking her to you."

Celd's face clouded over with rage. "He did not. He has not been back to the Lair for months. In fact, he is being sought as well as you. How you two are able to avoid the Sovereign's magic, and mine, is a mystery. Perhaps you could clear it up?"

Jaeger shrugged, shaking his head. "I...I didn't know I was being sought. I was punished. I thought that was the end of it. I am doing nothing to avoid detection."

Celd was quiet a moment, then brought his gaze back to meet Jaeger's. "And you are doing what out here?"

"Nothing," Jaeger lied. "Must I be doing something?"

Celd's gaze shifted to Vail. "A Bleeder?" he murmured, then suddenly lifted his head, as if sniffing the air. "And a witch!"

"No!" Jaeger moved forward, intent on doing whatever it took to stop Celd from hurting Vail.

"Oh, but he is," Celd said. "I can sense his magic. He's using it, right now. To..." He paused, his dark eyes narrowing, and then suddenly looked back at Jaeger. "To shield you!"

Jaeger's breath caught in his throat. Vail slid sideways to put even more distance between himself and the Vector. Celd chuckled and started toward the young man.

"No, Celd," Jaeger said, his voice firm and tight. "Leave him alone."

Celd stopped, looking from Vail to Jaeger and back. A slow smile touched at his thin lips. "Why, Jaeg, could it be? You and the boy? And here I thought that witch woman had claimed your heart. You even fought me for her. And now..." He chuckled. "Now, I find you enamored of a boy."

Jaeger flushed, but decided to play along, hoping it would dull Celd's interest. "That's right, Celd. I had no idea that a male could fulfill the same needs in me as a female."

Celd nodded, his gaze locked on Vail. "Yes, they can, can't they? And sometimes it's nice to have a variety. Come here, boy."

"No!" Jaeger snapped. He stepped between Celd and Vail.

The smile faded from Celd's face. "You defy me yet again, Jaeger? Didn't you learn anything?" He paused, suddenly thoughtful. "What exactly did old Darius do as punishment, anyway? You certainly don't look the worse for wear."

"He was quite thorough, Celd, trust me on that."

"Trust you? When Darius dotes on you like a son? And after what he's done in the Lair? I don't think so." He looked back at Vail. "Come here, boy," he said again.

Jaeger felt Celd's magic reach out toward Vail. He glanced over his shoulder to see the young man standing rigidly, eyes closed, fists clenched. He was fighting Celd's pull with all of his strength, but he was losing the battle.

In desperation, Jaeger looked back at Celd. He had no idea what Celd meant by "what Darius had done at the Lair," but it seemed to infuriate him. Jaeger decided to play on that, taking a wild chance that he was right. "Were I you, Celd, I wouldn't be wasting my time with the boy. Darius has Rhiannon and your child. His plans are anyone's guess."

Celd studied Vail a moment longer, then looked at Jaeger, uncertainty in his dark eyes. "You are right in that respect. Still, a Vector has to feed."

"Not on him."

Celd's eyebrows rose in surprise. "And you'll stop me? You'll again attack one of the Sovereign's Chosen? Do you value your life so little, Jaeger?"

Jaeger remained silent, not having an easy answer. Then he felt the unmistakable tingle of his shift beginning. The sun was rising.

"Vail!" he snapped. "Into the sunshine! Now!"

The boy wasted no time obeying. He darted from the overhang, even as Celd whirled toward him. Magic crackled outward. Jaeger redirected it, claiming it for his own. The resulting pain almost floored him. Vail disappeared into the yellow light of early morning. Celd spun to Jaeger, rage in his dark eyes.

"How dare you?" he seethed, then actually gasped as Jaeger shifted into the mountain cat.

Jaeger bounded past him and ran along the ledge. Magic struck the ground beside him, scattering dirt, rocks and sand in all directions. Jaeger swerved, keeping his course confusing, racing upward, and not allowing Celd a good target. At last, he was out of sight of the cave and Celd.

He slowed, panting, then looked for Vail. He saw the boy sagged against a boulder, shaking. Jaeger trotted up to him in alarm. Even in his cat form, Jaeger could smell the iron as it wafted from the boy's body. His magic use had been far too strong. Jaeger nudged up against him. Vail put out one arm, caught at Jaeger's strong body, then crumpled to the ground.

But Jaeger wouldn't let him rest. He nudged the young man, then growled, sending him to his feet in alarm.

"So," Vail mumbled, "now you're angry with me as well?"

Jaeger shook his head, took hold of Vail's pant leg, and pulled him forward. Vail sighed but followed. Jaeger set a frantic pace, wanting only to put some distance between them and Celd. He knew the Vector would come looking at nightfall, and he knew Celd's anger would not be dulled by a day spent confined to a small cave. Unfortunately, Celd had the benefit of Jaeger's pack and supplies.

He pushed Vail relentlessly, letting the young man stop only for brief rests before again urging him forward with a growl and a nudge. Finally, in late afternoon, Vail fell and did not get up. Jaeger stood over him, waiting, but Vail only looked up at him through teary eyes.

"I can't," he whispered. "I can't keep going, Jaeger. I tried. I just used too much magic. I can't go on."

Jaeger looked closely at the area they had reached. There wasn't much in the way of cover out here. No caves, no overhangs, just brush--thick tangles of it that looked impenetrable. Jaeger loped away from Vail to investigate several of the brushy groupings. In one, he saw a way to get into the center, away from direct view of anything flying overhead or running past.

Jaeger returned to Vail. The boy had almost fallen asleep, right where he lay. Jaeger nudged him awake, then again pulled at his clothing.

"No," Vail mumbled. "No, Jaeger. Leave me alone."

Jaeger pulled again. This time Vail struck out at him with an open hand. Jaeger growled, baring his teeth. Vail gasped and staggered to his feet.

"I'm sorry," he cried.

Jaeger ignored the terror in the voice and pushed Vail to walk. He led the boy to the brush, then crawled inside, hoping Vail would follow. He did.

"So, this is what you wanted," Vail said. "All right. I'm here. I did as you said. Now, it's time you helped me, Jaeger."

Jaeger balked. He remembered all too well what he had done to Rhiannon while in his cat form. He wasn't about to risk it with Vail. He shook his head and drew back.

Anger clouded Vail's young face. He reached out and grabbed a handful of Jaeger's fur. "You *will* help me! I used my magic to shield you earlier. I can use it to shield us both now. But I need to be bled first. Otherwise, I'll not have enough strength to keep us both hidden through the night. *I* don't want Celd to find us. I don't think you do either."

Jaeger could not dispute the words. He knew Celd. The Vector was likely to bleed Vail to death out of spite alone. Still, Jaeger hesitated, his own fear paralyzing him. He brought his gaze to Vail's. The young man stared back, a mixture of fatigue and determination in his blue eyes. Jaeger could not look away. He felt himself slipping into the blue depths, drawn to the boy, to his blood, to his own needs and desires.

Jaeger moved slowly, hypnotically, to Vail's side. Only when he was inches from the boy's neck did his gaze move from Vail's. Even then, it seemed it was because Vail allowed it. Driven by both his inner desire and by Vail's silent pleas, Jaeger lowered his mouth and sank his incisors into the boy's neck.

He drew on the blood, feeling it rush through him, warm him, and replenish his strength. Yet, there was a tight rein of control as well. He would not allow himself to hurt Vail. He would not allow his turbulent emotions to run wild.

Vail held to him, just as Rhiannon had done numerous times, and Jaeger was once more reminded of how much the siblings were alike. Thoughts of Rhiannon drove pain through his heart, worry through his gut. He had to find her, had to get to her before the baby was born. If he could not save himself from this life, at the least he could spare the child.

"There," Vail said quietly, pushing Jaeger aside. "There."

Jaeger sat back, mystified at this command Vail seemed to have over him. He watched, fascinated, as the bite wounds closed over and healed within moments.

Slowly, it dawned on him. Vail had again used the power associated with the Vector blood to command Jaeger to feed, and then again to bring his feeding to an end. Jaeger wasn't sure how he felt about that.

"I need to sleep for a while," Vail said. He lay down and curled into a fetal position. "Wake me at nightfall. I want a shield in place before the sun is gone. Promise me?"

Jaeger nodded and curled up beside Vail. In moments, they were both asleep.

Jaeger was pulled from sleep by the beginnings of his shift. Quickly, he roused Vail, hoping the boy would be able to work his magic while still half asleep. It took Vail only a second and a quick glance at the darkening sky, to throw a magic shield around them. It was securely in place by the time the last traces of sun disappeared, and Jaeger shifted. He eyed Vail with a grimace.

The young man smiled. "Why does that bother you? I saw you shift in the village. I saw you shift from cat to dragon when fighting those men. Yet, you still seem embarrassed by it."

Jaeger shrugged. "Shifting at will is one thing. Shifting by force is another." He was quiet for a moment. "I wish we hadn't lost the pack. We could do with some food and water."

Vail chuckled softly. "That's all right. I told you, I'm sick of rabbit. A night with only air suits me just fine."

"But will it still suit you come morning?"

"If not, then I'll be happy to once again accept rabbit."

Jaeger couldn't help but smile.

Vail glanced through their brushy enclosure at what was visible of the night sky. "I think we're close. I think we're very close to Rhiannon."

"How do you know? She could be anywhere on the coastline."

Vail shook his head. "No, she's close. I can...feel her, sense her. Somehow."

Jaeger regarded him thoughtfully. "That was a nice bit of magic you played out on me earlier."

Vail brought his gaze back to Jaeger's. "Magic?"

"Yes, you seduced me, Vail. Plain and simple. You made me feed on you despite my intentions not to."

"I did?" Vail seemed truly surprised.

"You did. And I suspect that when you return to your clan, Rachael will suddenly find you most attractive. But, then, so might a few dozen others. You'll be hard-pressed to decide which of the lovely young ladies you wish to be with."

"I will?" Vail mumbled. He was quiet for a long time, then suddenly grinned. "I will! But, no, it's Rachael I want. It's Rachael I've always wanted. No other."

Jaeger smiled and patted him on the shoulder. "And I am sure she wants you as badly as you want her."

"Why do you think that?"

"Why? Because you are a gifted, sensitive, caring and compassionate young man, Vail. I am proud to call you friend."

Vail's entire face lit up with delight. "Thank you, Jaeger, thank you so much. I am proud to call you friend, too. Or," he added with a teasing grin, "father."

Jaeger laughed. "I'm not that old as Vectors go." He shook his head and sat back to wait out the night. He wished he had a plan formulated, something he could use with confidence. But he had nothing. He had no idea how he would find Rhiannon, let alone keep Celd away from her.

Where did Darius fit into this? Why had he not taken Rhiannon back to the Lair as he'd said? What were his plans for her? And what had Darius done at the Lair that other Vectors should now be hunting him?

Jaeger had always cared a great deal for Darius. He had considered the Vector more than a friend. But now... Jaeger wasn't sure what to make of the whole situation. First, Darius' lying to him about changing him back to a Vector. Then lying about returning Rhiannon to Celd. Now, it seemed he was holed up in some beach cave with her, waiting for her to give birth to Celd's child. It just didn't make sense. This wasn't the Darius whom Jaeger knew and loved.

But, then, so much had changed in such a short time. He had come into his Growth. He had tasted human blood for the first time in his life. He had experienced sexual gratification with not just a woman, but with several men as well. And he had fallen desperately in love.

Yes, many things had changed, and if the events of the night before were any indication, much more was yet to change. Jaeger only hoped it was for the best.

Jaeger carefully watched Vail's face. The young man was beaded with sweat, his skin pale, his eyes glazed with fatigue. He was trembling, his entire body shuddering with concentration. Twice Jaeger had sensed a Vector nearby. With the shields around him, he couldn't be sure of the identity, but he took an educated guess.

Celd.

It was only moments until daybreak. If only Vail could hold his magic until then, he and Jaeger could move on, get farther away, and perhaps even find Rhiannon.

That thought, alone, sent chills through Jaeger. He could barely wait to see her again, to hold her, kiss her. But what really sent cold panic through him was her child. He didn't know if he possessed the strength of will to kill it. He didn't know if he should. He didn't know if Rhiannon would even allow it. A mother's love ran deep, even for a child conceived outside of love.

And what about Darius? Would he be there to stop Jaeger? To deny him access to Rhiannon and the child?

"Oh, by the saints!" Vail suddenly breathed. He opened his eyes. "I can't, Jaeger. I can't keep the shields up any longer."

"You must. Just for a few minutes more."

Tears swam in Vail's eyes, spilled over, and ran down his pale cheeks. "I can't," he repeated, his voice barely audible. "I'm sorry."

He crumpled at the same moment the shields did. Jaeger gasped and enveloped the young man in a tight embrace, half afraid Celd's magic would instantly claim him. *Please,* Jaeger begged mentally of the sun, *please rise.*

He sat in stony silence, cradling Vail in his arms, very aware of his own pounding heart, of Vail's tired breathing, of the intense scent of iron embracing them both. He knew Vail needed to be bled again, to be relieved of the excess iron that a full night of magic work had created, yet he was unwilling to do so until daylight once more provided a safe haven.

That he would have to bleed Vail as a mountain cat was a given. That he could control his cravings was not.

With Vail this weak and unable to project his own Vector magic, the control would be up to Jaeger. It was not something he wanted to think about at the moment. Right now, all he could concentrate on was keeping Vail with him and away from Celd.

A sigh of relief rushed from him as the first rays of sun caressed the lands. He lay his head against Vail's and closed his eyes. They had made it. At least, for one more night. Jaeger drew a quiet breath waiting for the shift.

Then, abruptly, Vector magic surrounded him. It sank dark, heavy claws into his mind and soul. It grabbed at him and tried to wrench him away from Vail. Jaeger bellowed in anger and held tighter, startling Vail to alertness.

The young man stared at him in terror; then, seeming to realize what was happening, he wrapped his arms about Jaeger's chest in a fierce hold. They were both sucked up in one powerful spell and whisked through time and space to land on a wide ledge outside a dark cave. The ocean waves snarled and hissed on the rocks below, sending spray high into the air. Each drop that touched Jaeger's skin stung like a nettle burn. He winced and got to his feet.

A voice hammered into his consciousness. A voice familiar and yet not what he expected. He turned, his eyes wide with disbelief. Darius stood on the ledge near the cave. He was motioning frantically to Jaeger.

"Inside! At once!" he snapped. "The boy, too!"

Jaeger helped Vail to his feet, and together they staggered into the cave. Rhiannon was lying on a cushion made of fir boughs and blankets. Her face was pale and sweaty, pain evident in her eyes. Jaeger gasped out a sob and fell to his knees beside her. She didn't seem surprised to see him, though she did let out a loud gasp as Vail dropped down beside Jaeger.

"Rhia!" Vail cried. "Thank the saints and goddesses!"

Jaeger reached for her hand, brought it to his lips, and kissed it gently. His mind was muddled. He didn't know what to make of anything.

He looked to Darius in question, but the Vector was watching the mouth of the cave. A second later, Celd appeared, shifting rapidly from the form of a hawk. He strode into the dim interior of the cave, rage darkening his face.

"What is the meaning of this?" he bellowed, his voice echoing from stone wall to stone wall.

Jaeger rose at once, wondering at the lack of respect Celd was showing to Darius. Even as a Chosen, Darius was still of a higher rank. Celd should have at least acknowledged that. But what was even more surprising was Darius' lack of upset over it. In fact, he seemed to be totally ignoring everything before him. Vail scampered to the other side of Rhiannon's bed and gripped her hand as if in reassurance. She looked up at Celd through eyes hazy with pain and fatigue.

"You're too late," she whispered, then let out a moan as a contraction tightened her abdomen.

"I am never too late," Celd snapped, then swung his gaze to Darius. "I asked you a question, old man! What is the meaning of this? How dare you take my hostess! How dare you keep her shielded from me all of this time!"

Again, Darius said nothing, but merely stared blankly at Celd. Jaeger frowned, and stepped towards the Elder, but Celd whirled on him, stopping him in mid stride.

"And you! You have written your own death warrant!" He spun out a magical attack sending Jaeger to his knees, gasping in agony.

"If my death is imminent," he managed, "at the least I will go out fighting." He brought his own magic forward and formed a Spell; but before he could cast it, the first rays of morning light sliced the horizon open.

"No!" Jaeger bellowed in fury and disbelief. "Darius! Do something!"

Celd roared with self-satisfied laughter as Jaeger became the mountain cat.

"So, Jaeg," he said coldly. "You've gotten yourself into quite a predicament, haven't you?"

Rhiannon let out a shriek of pain, drawing everyone's attention.

Celd smiled coldly. "My child will be a strong one," he snarled. "It gives its mother much pain. That is the way it should be. I shall give her more."

The words sent rage spiraling through Jaeger; and without thinking, he launched his muscular cat body at Celd. He hit the Vector in the chest, throwing both of them to the hard ground. Celd's breath rushed out with a grunt of surprise and pain. He quickly recovered and threw Jaeger off with a force fueled by magic.

Jaeger landed hard, rolled, and came again to his feet. The hip that had taken the arrow wound so many weeks ago throbbed mercilessly. He prepared himself for another attack on Celd even as Rhiannon once again screamed in pain. Jaeger dared a quick glance at her and Vail. The latter was white, his eyes enormous as he watched his sister prepare for birth.

Darius still hadn't moved. His eyes were glazed over as if his thoughts were far from what was happening in the cave before him. Jaeger returned his attention to Celd just in time.

The Vector had hoped to catch Jaeger off-guard and sent a powerful bolt of magic his way. Jaeger had just enough time to leap out of the way. He once again hurled himself at Celd, but the Vector was ready for him. He sidestepped and caught up Jaeger in a wicked web of magic, slamming him against the stone wall of the cave.

It took Jaeger a moment to get to his feet, to re-orient himself. He was tiring and in pain. His muscles ached, and old wounds reminded him of their presence. His limp was more pronounced as he stepped forward once again.

Celd seemed more in control, stronger than Jaeger had ever seen him. He wondered why, if it was a side benefit of being a Chosen. Then again, Celd had not just spent the last few months trekking across an inhospitable land. And Celd was not a halfling. A halfling, distracted now, as the woman he loved writhed in agony.

Her shrill cries echoed in the caves, tearing into Jaeger's heart. He wanted to be with her, to help her, comfort her. More than that, he wanted to remove Celd from the picture. He watched, still dazed, as Celd moved closer to Rhiannon. The thought of him touching her again drove insane jealousy and hate through Jaeger. A growl escaped him as he crouched for another attack.

Water. The word drifted into Jaeger's thoughts, and he turned his gaze on Darius. The Vector was watching him, but made no movement to help either him or Rhiannon. Water? Jaeger shook his head in confusion, even as Rhiannon cried out again.

Celd stood over her, a smirk on his face. Rhiannon glared up at him, gritting her teeth against the pain that wracked her body. Vail seemed paralyzed by both his fear of Celd and his empathy for what Rhiannon was going through. When Celd's gaze moved to him, Vail caught his breath and backed away. Jaeger growled in warning.

Celd spun on him. "Don't threaten me, Jaeger!" he seethed. "I could kill you with one touch! But I think I'll let you witness the birth first. I want you to see what a wonderful hostess I picked. This woman will serve me well. And when I am done with her, this boy will take her place."

Jaeger roared in fury, but it was Vail who reacted. He bolted from his position, leapt over Rhiannon's body, and flung himself at Celd. The attack caught the Vector by surprise, and he staggered backward. Jaeger used the opportunity to dart forward, and place himself behind Celd's legs. The Vector fell over him, landing hard on the stone. He bellowed in pain, trying to right himself. Jaeger used his massive jaws, his wickedly sharp teeth, and tore into Celd's neck.

Celd retaliated with a wild, random attack of magic. Jaeger heard Vail shriek and scuffle away, but he would not relax his grip on Celd's neck. He finally understood what Darius meant. The water. The water crashing and snarling below the ledge. The water heavy with stinging salt, alive with full daylight.

Wicked bolts of magic slammed against him as he dragged Celd from the cave. At the same time, something enveloped Jaeger, keeping the agony at a bearable level. Jaeger wondered if it was Rhiannon or Vail shielding him, but had little time to dwell on it.

Celd writhed in agony as the sunlight touched his hair, caught at his skin, and tore into his senses. He struggled to free himself from Jaeger's grasp. Jaeger held firm, though his strength was rapidly waning. His fur was singed completely off where Celd's magic had ripped into him. His hip was alive with agony, hampering his movements. He knew he would never be able to push Celd over the cliff. He would have to drag him over.

Rhiannon's screams turned from those of pain to those of terror, as she connected with Jaeger's thoughts.

No, Jaeger! Don't! Please, don't!

The despair in the words cut into Jaeger's concentration, and Celd wrested free, his blood dripping to the ground. His wound began to heal itself at once, though his skin was blistering from the sun's touch. He staggered to his feet, gasping, and slammed Jaeger with a magic jolt so intense it sent him sprawling to the dirt. Jaeger attempted to rise but could not summon the strength to do so. Still, he would not give up. He dragged his battered body toward Celd, roaring as bolt after bolt tore into him, sending his muscles into spasms of pure agony.

He smelled his own burning fur and flesh, knew he bled from dozens of wounds. Still, he crawled forward.

"You'll pay, Jaeger!" Celd screamed. "You'll pay for everything!" He delivered one last searing bolt of magic.

Jaeger collapsed, his breathing rasping in his chest. Rhiannon's screams reached a new intensity, and he knew that she had given birth to the child. As did Celd.

The Vector spun toward the cave, abandoning his attack on Jaeger. He took two steps forward, then gasped as Vail abruptly bolted from the cave, his scream of rage and defiance shattering the morning chill.

The young man caught Celd with both arms, never breaking his forward momentum, and the two men disappeared over the cliff.

Jaeger stared at the empty space where the two men had been. Then, his roar of disbelief and despair spun into the air. He closed his eyes and sprawled on the hard ground, willing death to claim him as well. However, it was not death that touched him. It was Darius' magic. It surrounded him, stroked him, and caressed him with love. It swept him up in its powerful embrace and transported him to a place of peace and healing. He felt safe and secure. And loved. More so than he had felt since he was a small child. Images of his parents were strong and constantly present. They comforted him, brought him a sense of peace, and eased the turmoil in his shattered spirit.

How long he stayed in the healing trance, he didn't know. But, finally, he shuddered and opened his eyes to find that he was once more in Vector form, lying in the cool darkness of the cave. Rhiannon lay within arms' reach, holding the baby well wrapped and suckling at her breast.

Jaeger stared at her, at the child, his mind dully registering that the child was drinking human milk.

"Jaeger?" The voice was soft and familiar.

Jaeger sat up so fast his head spun. Vail was sitting near a small fire, tending to a piece of roasting meat. He looked whole and healthy, unscathed by his plunge into the rocky surf. Jaeger frowned, shaking his head. He closed his eyes, opened them again. Nothing had changed.

Rhiannon smiled at him as Vail approached them. "Jaeger?" he said again. "How are you feeling?"

"How am I...me..." Jaeger stared at him in shock. "Me? You! How did you...I mean, you went over the cliff!"

Vail chuckled. "I did, didn't I? Well, thank the saints I can swim fairly well."

"But the rocks," Jaeger said. "You couldn't have survived the fall."

"Not on my own, no," Vail replied. "But I had a little help."

"Help?"

"From you. From your blood. And from Darius." He gestured.

Jaeger turned, startled. Darius approached from the gloom of the caves. He wore a small smile, and he gestured toward the baby. "He's a handsome boy, Jaeger. You should be proud."

"Proud?" Jaeger looked again at Rhiannon and the child. "Proud?"

"Here." Rhiannon took the child from her breast and held him out to Jaeger. "Hold your son, Jaeger."

The words took several moments to register. Jaeger shook his head. "No. The child is--"

"Is yours," Rhiannon interrupted. "I was already with child when Celd tried to implant the embryo. This is your son, Jaeger, not his. And your son has had breast milk. He has no Vector tendencies now. He will not need blood to survive. Here, hold your son."

"Go on," Darius encouraged, smiling.

Jaeger took the small child in his arms, staring at the wide-open, trusting eyes. He gently traced the baby's round face, touched the tiny fingers. They curled about his in a grip that surprised him.

"But how?" he whispered. "I don't understand."

"I suspected. Darius knew," Rhiannon said. "When I told him that I believed I carried your child, he took me away to keep me safe from Celd. You couldn't know, else Celd would be able to follow, to track you, to read your thoughts. It was enough of a strain for Darius just to keep this place hidden from Celd."

Jaeger looked up at Darius. "Is this why you were being sought? Celd said you had done something in the Lair. Darius, are you in trouble because you helped me?"

At that, Darius chuckled. "Trouble? I am far too old to get into trouble."

Jaeger paused, his gaze back on the child. "Why did you deceive me?" he finally asked. "Why did you promise Rhiannon that I would return to my Vector form in exchange for her returning to Celd? Why did you trap me in an animal's body like that?"

It was Vail who answered. "Simple," he said with a shrug. "So you could travel in the daylight, as well as at night."

Jaeger frowned in confusion. "So I could travel? Then you wanted me to search for Rhiannon?"

"Of course, I did, but I had to let you do it on your own. I couldn't bring you here without bringing Celd here as well," Darius replied. "It was much safer for Rhiannon to have you gallivanting about the countryside, leading Celd on a merry chase."

Jaeger fixed his gaze on Darius. "Do you realize how much anger burned inside me these past few months? I hated you, Darius. I hated what you did to me, how you took me away from Rhiannon. I wanted to hunt you down, make you pay for the pain you put me through."

"I know," Darius said softly. "And I am sorry for that, but there was no other way. If you had known my plans, all would have been lost at the beginning."

"And the Sovereign did expect a punishment be dealt," Rhiannon put in.

Mention of the Sovereign sent panic once more coursing through Jaeger. He turned a wild gaze on Darius. "And now what awaits me? A Chosen has been killed. Because of me. A child is stripped of Vector heritage. Because of me. Darius, I--"

"It's been handled," Darius interrupted.

"Handled? How? By somehow evading the Sovereign's reach? Celd said we were doing that, both of us, but I don't know how. And I can't be on the run for the rest of my life." His shoulders sagged and tears stung his eyes as he gazed at his son. "I cannot condemn this child to a life like that, Darius. Rhiannon, I want you and Vail to take our son back to your clan. I want you to raise him there, away from me, from who and what I am."

Rhiannon's chin quivered, and she reached out to place one cool hand on his cheek. "We don't have to run anymore, Jaeger. The Sovereign no longer seeks you. In fact, the Sovereign and his followers approve of you and your new family."

Jaeger stared at her in confusion.

Vail grinned and gestured at Darius. "Meet the Sovereign," he said softly.

A gasp escaped Jaeger. "What?" he breathed. "No, that's not possible. Darius, you--"

Darius chuckled. "It is as Vail states. I am the new Sovereign. Sovereign

Cardiss has been dead for many months. High Chancellor Riden has been lying to us all. All I needed to do was to prove it. There were quite enough Vectors in residence at the Lair to see to it that the High Chancellor was ousted from his position. Still, he did not go without a fight."

Jaeger stared at him, stunned. "*This* was the trouble you were causing in the Lair?" he cried. "A coup?"

"I told you I did not agree with Cardiss' ways, or with those of Riden. They took my son from me. I was not going to let them take you and your son as well."

Sudden anger engulfed Jaeger. "Then why didn't you help me? You have magic enough! Why did you allow me, Vail, and Rhiannon to suffer from Celd's magic? Or was that part of my punishment as well?"

Rhiannon reached out and placed her hand on Jaeger's arm. "He did help you, Jaeger. He shielded you as best he could."

Jaeger snorted in disbelief. "It didn't feel much like a shield," he snarled, then looked away when Darius shot him a glance of disapproval. "I apologize, Elder, it's just that...well, I know you have more power than that. Why didn't you use it to help me?"

Darius sighed. "I did, Jaeger. But it was not only Celd and his magic I was dealing with. Celd and his father were both Chosen. In addition, his father was the High Chancellor. They had combined their magic in an attempt to rule the Lair. They killed Cardiss; but because they had so few followers, they could not let his death be known. They allowed the Vectors to believe Cardiss was yet alive while they gathered supporters to protect their new regime. Few sided with them, but, joined together as they were, Celd and his father were extremely powerful. In the end, it was that thirst for power that proved their downfall. When Celd died, so did Riden. Celd could not break his connection with his father in time. Pity."

Jaeger stared at him, understanding the implications. Celd had probably tried, and was prevented from doing so by Darius. Jaeger drew a deep breath, then looked over as Vail suddenly groaned in despair.

The color had drained from his face. "But then...I'm to blame! I...I killed Celd, and...the High Chancellor!"

Darius nodded, though a slight smile played at his lips. "Yes, and I am very grateful for your help."

Vail's eyes widened, but he seemed at a loss for words. Jaeger studied him a moment, then returned his attention to Darius.

"Why?" The question was simple, yet asked so much.

Darius hesitated before sitting beside Jaeger. He reached for the infant and cradled the child in his arms. For long moments, he said nothing, his gaze on the baby. When he finally spoke, his voice was soft. "Do you remember what I said about my son?"

Jaeger nodded. "You said that Cardiss took him from you. That your son had loved a human, just as my father did."

"My son," Darius said, lifting his gaze to meet Jaeger's, "*was* your father."

The words stunned Jaeger, left him speechless.

Darius gave a sad smile. "Of all the children who are a part of me, he was perhaps more so. I can't explain it, Jaeger, I only accept it."

"Perhaps," Rhiannon said quietly, "you loved his mother."

Darius seemed startled by the idea. He looked at the infant. "Yes," he admitted after a long moment. "Yes, I did." He turned his gaze back on Jaeger. "And I love his son."

"Then that's why you looked after me all of those years?" Jaeger mumbled. "Not as a friend of my father's, but as my grandfather? Why didn't you tell me?"

"With my rebel tendencies, I didn't want to implicate you in any way. It was better for Riden to believe you were far from my thoughts. Had he known of my love for you, he could have used that to quash any uprising against him. I would never have let him torture you to stop me."

The mere idea sent chills racing through Jaeger. "I appreciate that," he murmured. "But, Rhiannon and the baby, you risked your life to help them."

Darius nodded. "Again, had Riden discovered the baby's true heritage, it could have been used against me. It was in my own best interest to keep Rhiannon well-hidden until she gave birth."

"Best interest?" Jaeger repeated. "Again, practicality over emotion."

Rhiannon grimaced. "Don't you understand, Jaeger? Practicality may guide us, but it is emotion that sustains us. It was Darius' love for you, for your father, that set the coup in motion. It was the Vectors' desire to choose their own mates that gave Darius supporters. It was love for my own people that led me to offer them to the Vectors."

"Then the arrangement has been accepted?" Jaeger asked.

"It has," Darius replied. "But it is an arrangement of choice. Neither the Vectors nor the Bleeders will be forced to take part."

Jaeger looked at the child in his arms. "And the baby? Is he a Bleeder as well?"

Rhiannon's smile lit up her small face. "No. He is immune. He is the first child in our clan's history that is so. And he has his father to thank."

"Me?"

Darius chuckled. "You. Although it is too early to tell just what made it possible. It could be that whatever is in a Vector's bite that cleanses the iron from a Bleeder, is also present in his seed. Or, it could be a unique result of your halfling state."

"It doesn't matter," Rhiannon said. "The important thing is that my people will no longer have to suffer and die. No longer will your people have to prey on the unwilling. It is our gift of blood to you. It is your gift of life to us."

Jaeger tore his gaze from the baby and met Rhiannon's. For a long moment, he could only stare into the blue depths of her eyes.

Then, he leaned forward and claimed her lips with his.

You can find ALL our books up on our website at:

http://www.writers-exchange.com

all our fantasy novels:

http://www.writers-exchange.com/category/genres/fantasy/

JennaKay Francis has been writing since she was 12 years old. She has written in many different genres - science fiction, childrens, mainstream, poetry - but truly found her voice and love in fantasy. She writes fantasy adventure, fantasy romance, dark fantasy and children's picture books.

Her first official publication was a children's poem that was the Grand Prize winner in a contest sponsored by Half-Price Books. Her prize was a $500.00 gift certificate at Half Price Books: something she took great delight in spending. She has been published in several local newsletters, several print magazines, as well as numerous online magazines in both fiction and non-fiction.

Jenna lives in the beautiful Pacific Northwest with her husband, their three delightful children, two wild cats, a chihuahua that thinks he's really a dog, one rat, one anole and a several tanks of tropical fish, frogs and newts.

Oh, yeah, and a forest full of elves, fairies and magic.

JennaKay was also Writers Exchange's Senior editor for many years.

You can keep track of all her books on her author page:

http://www.writers-exchange.com/Jennakay-Francis/

If you want to read more about other books by this author, they are listed on the following pages...

Blood Bred Series

{Fantasy: Vampire}

Book 1: Gift of Blood

Jaeger needs blood. Half Vector, half human, newly coming of age, Jaeger is now drawn to human blood for the first time in his already long life.

Rhiannon, a witch, has too much iron in her blood to safely live. She wants to propose a partnership with the Vectors, but, before she can approach them, she's attacked and left for dead beneath a pier. Jaeger finds her unconscious and bleeding. Fighting against the lure of her blood, he takes her to a place of safety instead. His actions set them both on a course of pain, hunger, terror and love. Can he save her from himself?

Publisher: http://www.writers-exchange.com/Gift-Of-Blood/

Book 2: From the Heart

Baris has everything: A wife he worships, a child he adores, a life of comfort and security. But his idyllic existence changes suddenly and dramatically, with no explanation. Anika, his wife, shuns him and orders him to leave her side. His child claims his mother is not really his mama. And Dierdre, a devastatingly beautiful young woman slides into Baris' life with seduction on her mind.

When Baris attempts to help his wife, she flees, leaving him alone with their son and Dierdre. To add to his agony, the child is bitten by a poisonous snake and Baris has no choice but to take him to the Lair to save his life. Once reunited with Dierdre, the pair set off in search of Anika. But, as the days turn to weeks with no sign of his wife, Baris must accept the possibility that she has no wish to be found.

As his life grows increasingly entangled with Dierdre's, he makes the mistake of feeding on a young man addicted to a powerful drug called Hack. Baris is soon addicted as well and must struggle to reclaim everything that he once held dear...or die.

Publisher: http://www.writers-exchange.com/From-the-Heart/

Book 3: New Beginnings

A powerful Vector roams the dark alleys and streets searching for his next victim. But he he's not interested in those with normal blood--only those whose veins runs blood thick with the highly-addictive drug Hack. If Adan can't find someone who's just ingested the potent drug, he has no compunction about using his powers to coerce them to do so before he feeds.

For Vector Sovereign Darius, Adan has become a problem he needs to fix...

Publisher: http://www.writers-exchange.com/New-Beginnings/

Free Spirit

{Fantasy Romance}

Diesa de Tyronmen escapes from a brutal master only to be sold to an elf. Though mesmerized by his beauty, Diesa struggles for her freedom...and against her own growing love for her new master. Was she purchased only to win a wager? And, as her mother had claimed, will an elf claim her heart with his words, her very soul with his touch?

Publisher: http://www.writers-exchange.com/Free-Spirit/

The Faery Sickness

{Fantasy Romance}

Vala Kalei was saved from death by the fae but condemned by her own neighbors. When she goes to the faery realm and retrieves the babies that have been dying, she opens up another world filled with mystery, pain, heartache...and love.

Publisher: http://www.writers-exchange.com/The-Faery-Sickness/

Guardians of Glede Universe:

Beginnings Series

{Fantasy: Young Adult}

When the balance of power is threatened in the land of Glede, the powerful Triskelion calls for its master.

Book 1: The Triskelion

The Triskelion, a powerful magical amulet, once torn into two parts to protect the world of Glede, now must be found and re-united to save Glede. Two boys are summoned by the magic of the Triskelion to perform this dangerous task -Treyas Beckering, a 14 year old elf from Bailiwycke in the west; and 13 year old Jannson van Tannen, the newly orphaned King of Odora Dava to the east. Both will endure more than they ever thought possible, and both will become men in the process.

Publisher: http://www.writers-exchange.com/The-Triskelion/

Book 2: Dark Prince

Prince Rugan Merripen, once thought to be the rightful master of the Triskelion's magic, was cast aside by the medallion itself when it chose his half-brother Treyas Beckering as master. Now Rugan is on a quest to regain the magic and power he thinks is rightfully his. Befriended and manipulated by Vaalde, an evil sorcerer who has only his own goals in mind, Rugan attempts to drain Glede of elfin magic. Once gone, only sorcery magic will remain and Vaalde can then rule the world. It is up to King Jansson and Treyas to stop him and restore the balance of magic once again. Each boy will face what seem to be insurmountable odds, and both will discover that friends are there to depend on in times of travail. And Treyas will move towards a destiny that he never envisioned.

Publisher: http://www.writers-exchange.com/Dark-Prince/

Book 3: Sorcerer's Pool

Firmly embedded into Prince Rugan's mind, the sorcerer Vaalde once more manipulates Prince Rugan into wresting the Triskelion magic from Treyas Beckering Merripen, now the Crown Prince of Lidgerwood. This time Vaalde spirits King Jansson van Tannen and Treyas to Karsaba, a land void of magic and the ability to drain memory. Three days outside of magic and their memories will be wiped clean. Unfortunately for Vaalde, King Kyel Sylvain has hitched a ride. The black elf, reknowned for his magical prowess will prove to be a formidable adversary. But will Jansson and Treyas survive the strange power of Karsaba or will they lose everything that makes them who they are?

Publisher: http://www.writers-exchange.com/Sorcerers-Pool/

Book 4: Dragons of Mere Odain

Far away in the land of Mere Odain, a dragon calls out for help to her master--Pepin Merripen, now living as the son of Crown Prince Treyas Merripen and his wife, Cynthe. Pepin must answer, or die. Shocked and terrified, Treyas gathers his closest friends, and goes to Mere Odain. But the country is in turmoil. An ethnic cleansing is going on--any black or brown skinned person must die. Treyas is determined to save his young son's life even if it means taking on the whole of the Keltin Empire and ending a war 40 years in the making.

Publisher: http://www.writers-exchange.com/Dragons-of-Mere-Odain/

Book 5: Dragon Master

Pepin Merripen learns that the two countries that had promised to protect the dragons, his dragons, have withdrawn their forces. Furious at this betrayal, he goes to Karsaba to take council with Mere Odain's young Queen. Although his father is willing to let Pepin resolve this situation, he soon finds out that Pepin has disappeared. Treyas follows his son's trail, but it ends where magic begins.

Increasingly worried, Treyas attempts to follow the magical trail and ends up in Northern Karsaba. It soon becomes apparent that he has more to deal with than a disgruntled runaway youth. A powerful magiker claiming to be Pepin's birth mother has summoned him, and she will stop at nothing to see his control over the dragons become her own. With Pepin at her command, and thereby his dragons, she intends to rule not only Karsaba, but any land she chooses. It is up to Treyas and his friends to make sure that doesn't happen. But will Treyas lose his son to the powerful pull of the dragons?

Publisher: http://www.writers-exchange.com/Dragonmaster/

Book 6: For the Love of Dragons

Pepin Merripen, now a young man of fourteen, has forged a strong bond with the elves. So when Queen El'leigh of Mere Odain informs him that the dragons have disappeared, he is torn between his allegiance and his love for the dragons. Still, he is steadfast in his loyalty to his father, Treyas Merripen, and refuses El'leigh's request to join her in the search.

Furious, El'leigh sends Pepin's love, Nila, to the wilds of South Kelta, the last known place of the dragons. As she suspected, Pepin quickly follows before any harm befalls Nila. No sooner have the two young lovers arrived in Kelta, than they are captured by Keltin warriors, who quickly ascertain that they have the DragonMaster in their grasp. And if they can force Pepin to make the dragons do their bidding, they'll regain their lost advantage in Mere Odain. All they have to do is use Nila as incentive.

Publisher: http://www.writers-exchange.com/For-The-Love-Of-Dragons/

Guardians of Glede Universe Continued:

Next Generation Series

{Fantasy: Young Adult}

Return to the land of Glede for new adventures with the next generation!

Book 1: Caves of Challenge

Their heads filled with stories of adventures spun by their father and uncles, Princes Vantann and Thomlin Merripen decide to have an adventure of their own. Through an old book, they learn of the Caves of Challenge. If they can survive the challenges within the caves, they will emerge as men.

Blackmailed by their young friend, Shuri, the boys agree to take her along. Before they trio has a chance to adequately prepare, however, they are sent to the Caves by haphazard magic. Once there, Shuri and Vantann are captured by War Gnomes, while Thomlin is lost in a dark swamp. His only consolation is that, somehow, he has snagged King Jansson van Tannen on the magic strand.

Jansson is reassuring, telling Thomlin that there will be a rescue party sent out and all they need do is wait. But the rescue party is having trouble of their own, and they find much more than they bargained for in the Caves. The question now becomes, who will be forced to stay in the Caves of Challenge forever.

Publisher: http://www.writers-exchange.com/Caves-of-Challenge/

Book 2: Blood Sacrifice

Tormented with guilt over the happenings in the Caves of Challenge, Prince Vantann Merripen watches over his siblings with a critical, judgmental and sometimes violent scrutiny. Prince Thomlin finally rebels and accidentally sets the course for an even more dangerous adventure than the one he and his brother endured in the Caves. Swept into a land that demonizes the second-born of twins, forbids magic, and is currently being terrorized by a coven of Nydiri, the twins very survival is threatened.

Any use of magic carries the penalty of death. Contact with the coven means the same, for the Nydiri are actively seeking twins to complete a powerful spell they intend to weave at the height of a mysterious orange moon. And elvin twins are especially prized.

Publisher: http://www.writers-exchange.com/Blood-Sacrifice/

Book 3: The Coven

Pepin reclaims his title as DragonMaster, not fully understanding the ramifications of such a move. Is his allegiance with the elves, or with Mere Odain? The announcement of his decision couldn't have come at a worse time – the Crown Prince is to leave the next day on a diplomatic visit to Dalziel.

Once in Dalziel, things rapidly begin to fall apart. Politically, Kyel and Jansson are at each other's throats, Vantann and Thomlin make friends in the wrong places, and Treyas finds out that his SoulMate and squire, Druce Sinclair, suffers from a horribly painful and incurable disease.

To top it off, Treyas discovers that Dalziel has been overrun with Nydiri with the power of Illusion in their grasp.

When Vantann, Thomlin and others disappear, Treyas must find a way to free the captives and destroy the Nydiri threat once and for all...

Publisher: http://www.writers-exchange.com/The-Coven/

Book 4: Fire Stone

Stranded after a river float trip goes horribly wrong, Brann van Tannen and his friends Tavin, Elek and Janna are caught by slave traders. To make matters worse, on board the barge are three trolls, descendants of the tribe that destroyed Mayfaire and killed Brann's grandfather. Brann will need to rely on all of the strength, wisdom and courage his father instilled in him while their lives are changed beyond wildest imagination.

Publisher: http://www.writers-exchange.com/Fire-Stone/

Book 5: The Fane Queen

Attempting to escape the past can have devastating consequences...

Ask Tavin Sylvain, who is trying to forget all about the abuse he suffered at the hands of the trolls six months earlier.

Ask Kitiara, who would like to escape her sordid past in Kartonn, where she was known as the Princess of Pleasure.

Or ask King Jansson van Tannen, who would like nothing better than to keep his family intact and not have to face the possibility of losing one of his own beloved children to fate.

When the past rears its ugly head, all three are thrown into turmoil. Tavin, Brann and Kitiara are lost in Karsaba, without magic, without direction, without hope. And in the middle of a troll invasion. In a race against time, King Jansson and King Kyel gather their closest friends and allies to find the children before the trolls find them first.

Publisher: http://www.writers-exchange.com/The-Fane-Queen/

Book 6: Battle for Argathia

A desperate plea for help, written on a scroll and sent with magic, falls into the wrong hands, and with a few misplace words, Treyas' young daughter activates the spell, sending her and her friends to a world controlled by the Albino.

The Albino, not content with being dictator of only one world, now has a hostage--and one of royal pedigree--with which to extend his empire. It is up to Treyas and his companions to stop the Albino and free the world he has claimed as his own.

Publisher: http://www.writers-exchange.com/Battle-for-Argathia/

Guardians of Glede Universe Continued:

Reckonings Series

{Fantasy: Young Adult}

Return to the land of Glede during a time when the Nydiri intend to destroy not only Treyas but the whole of the elven empire.

Book 1: Dukker's Revenge

Elek is missing and Dukker has returned. The Nydiri will not stop until not only Treyas is destroyed but the whole of the elven empire. When the palace is infiltrated, chaos ensues. Floy, the son of a visiting dignitary, becomes an unwitting pawn in Dukker's plans. Through him, Dukker captures three of the royal youth.

Treyas and his companions set out to rescue the young people, but their TravelSpell is severely compromised, sending them in different directions. They will all need to rely on new friends, and a powerful, mysterious dagger, to set things right and defeat the Nydiri.

Publisher: http://www.writers-exchange.com/Rukkers-Revenge/

Nitesh

{Fantasy Romance}

Thalassa, a sea-witch, is captured when the warlord Rhaeven sends his troops to her small village. After the hard life she's already lived, she's resigned to her fate. Married at a young age to an abusive man she doesn't love, she's secretly glad to see her husband die. Now, pregnant, enslaved and stricken with a deadly disease, she only waits for her own death to release her from the torment that is life.

Elfin Crown Prince of Diraenia, Terran, must choose a mate and produce an heir before his thirtieth birthday or risk forfeiting the crown to his youngest brother Unwin. Time is running out. Terran is twenty-nine, his fiancee is dead, and he believes Unwin responsible despite the lack of proof. To make matters worse, Terran's other brother Sinclair has disappeared, and Terran fears the worst.

Bothered by a strange, haunting beat of drums no one can hear but Terran, the Crown Prince thoughts continually turn to a brief encounter he shared with a young woman from Zal. For three days, he'd walked her back to her village, delivering her to her pre-ordained life there. For three days, he fell in love with the wife of a woman who could never be his. When he returned to his own palace, he'd seen the emptiness and despair of his own life.

The drums call to Terran until he can longer deny his own need to revisit the village where he'd fallen in love. If he sees Thalassa one last time, can he make himself let go?

Publisher: http://www.writers-exchange.com/Nitesh/

If you want to read more about other Fantasy novels by this publisher, they are listed on...

http://www.writers-exchange.com/category/genres/fantasy/

You can find ALL our books up on our website at:

http://www.writers-exchange.com